I0571183

Critter Sitter Chronicles 2

4th of July Parade

by

Valerie Ondrejko

Illustrated by

Haley Berlak

NORELLA PRESS, LLC. /
ELKHORN, NE

Critter Sitter Chronicles2

4th of July Parade

Copyright © 2019 by Valerie Ondrejko

All rights reserved. No part of this publication may be reproduced, distributed or transmitted in any form or by any means, including photocopying, recording, or other electronic or mechanical methods, without the prior written permission of the publisher, except in the case of brief quotations embodied in critical reviews and certain other noncommercial uses permitted by copyright law.

For more information contact:
Norella Press, LLC.
norellapress@gmail.com/www.norellapress.com

Publisher's Note: This is a work of fiction. Names, characters, places, and incidents are a product of the author's imagination. Locales and public names are sometimes used for atmospheric purposes. Any resemblance to actual people, living or dead, is completely coincidental.

Copyright © 2019 Valerie Ondrejko
Elkhorn / Valerie Ondrejko — First Edition
Printed in the United States of America
ISBN 978-0-9983628-6-1

Monday, June 28

GRRR! There was no way I was I going to let know-it-all Ashley get under my skin today! Her friendly chit-chat was just a sneaky way to find out our plans. Plus, she just wanted to rub it in my face how awesome her Fourth of July parade float was going to be. But I had no control over my reaction.

When I saw Ashley peddling by on my way to walk Max, I really wanted to tell her about riding The Scorpion with

Ryan; that would shut her up. I would swing my hair like she does and say, "Well, when Ryan and I were riding The Scorpion, he mentioned how he loves Moo Moo's Creamery and I plan to share my winnings with him." But that would backfire. She would know I had a major crush on him, then blab her mouth to the entire grade. She'd find a way to make the news spread, even though we were on summer vacation.

Then she'd say to me, "Does he know how you and Maia were in his house?" BOOM! She'd have me by the throat. I hadn't told Ryan that we were his fish sitters. I didn't want to freak him out or anything. Not to mention that I overfed his fish and almost made them explode. So, for now, I had to let Ashley flap her lips about how her Fourth of July float was going to be the most perfect show of patriotism, and if I wanted to win, I better join her team. Which would mean she'd want me to drop Maia to the curb. She does not know the first thing about friendship and loyalty.

"Seriously Paige, I have access to the best carpenter in town. He's going to help me build a...well if you don't want to be on my team then I'm not going to spill all the good details," she snorted.

"Can't. We're almost done with ours already, so like we can't just join your team now," I said. That was a total lie. We hadn't even come up with an idea for our float. Now, I was panicking.

"Oh, well I was just talking about you. Maia just wouldn't fit the theme of my float," Ashley said as she peddled along.

"And what theme is that?" I asked.

"Well, I can't just give away my secrets," she said and tossed her hair.

That girl is so vague AND so vain. She is on the top of my GRRR list.

Ashley needed to just keep on riding. "Okay, well, I have to get to my dog walking. See ya later, Ashley," I said and darted across to the other side of the street.

I thought she was going to speed off, but then she flung her hair over her other shoulder as she turned back and said, "Well, if you don't want to be partners, I'll have to find someone else like Ryan Shootie, he said he'd do it." Then she peddled as fast as she could.

I froze and gaped at her in total amazement. How dare she! Now she was definitely under my skin, like a biting, annoying gnat. My mom would say, "Let it go. It's not worth it to get so mad." But, what if she wasn't doing this just to get me mad? What if she liked Ryan, too? This was bad. Real bad!

"Ick!" A bug flew into my mouth. Gross! I spat into the grass. Then again. I couldn't tell if it was out or if I swallowed it. Ohh, if only I could spit that bug right at Ashley. She had my blood boiling.

When I got to Mrs. Henderson's house, Maia was waiting for me. "How come you didn't get Max yet?" I asked.

"My mom just dropped me off," Maia said.

"Let me see, let me see," I said.

Maia smiled a weird smile to show off her new braces. They were turquoise. "Cool color. Do they hurt?"

"They don't hurt yet. They just feel strange," Maia said.

"You should have done red, white, and blue for the Fourth of July parade," I said shoving her shoulder with mine.

"Oh yea, that would have been cool," Maia agreed.

"OMG just wait till I tell you this. I just saw Ashely and she said she is going to ask Ryan to be on her float team. How rude is that?" I growled.

Mrs. Henderson appeared at the door. "I thought I heard you girls."

Maia jogged up the steps and took Max's leash. I waved and stayed put. He is still on my GRRR list too.

Max darted down the steps on his three legs and came right up to me. He barked. OMG, his black gums were showing as the spit dripped from his fangs.

"Why is he barking at me already?" I said backing away.

Maia tugged on his leash. "You always carry the you-know-what. You don't have them. I bet he knows. He is really smart," Maia said.

"Smart? Yea, right. Smart enough to know he can gobble me up in a minute," I argued.

"Would you stop. You better go get them. Hurry," Maia said.

Max did always cooperate better when he knew I had his treats. I slowly walked away from him still keeping an eye on his open jaw. GRRR yourself Max, I thought. I ran up to the door and whispered to Mrs. Henderson, "I need his treats."

"Oh yes, dear. Here you go," Mrs. Henderson said and pulled the treats out of her apron pocket. I hope she doesn't keep cookies she gives us in those pockets too, I thought. ICK.

Max pulled Maia along and I ran to catch up. Maia said, "You know what? I bet Ryan will be at his boat. He won't even be here for the Fourth of July parade."

"Exactly. Ashley thinks she knows everything and wants to start trouble," I agreed. Then I thought, Ryan probably wouldn't be at the parade. DARN IT!

"So, what are we going to do for our float?" Maia asked.

"I don't know. We better think fast because we only have a few days left," I said.

"What if we make a float that can attach to our bikes and we pull it behind us?" Maia said.

"Maybe we tie Max to it, and he can pull it. He is always full of energy," I said.

"You're seriously going to want Max with us in the parade?" Maia looked at me like I was crazy.

"I was just kidding."

Max looked back at me. I had a feeling he knew what I was saying.

"What about a boat? It can be like the pilgrims coming over to start the country," I said.

"That reminds me too much of Thanksgiving," Maia said. "We can dress up in some kind of costume."

"That would be way too embarrassing. No way." I shook my head emphasizing my dislike of the idea.

"Then we should do something that relates to us," Maia said and stopped walking. Max was doing his doggie business.

"But what can we do that relates to us that other people will understand. I mean, we can't do a movie and makeup float. Although that would be cool," I said and smiled at the thought.

"They're having the movie in the park on the big wall there, remember? Maybe we have a huge popcorn float in the shape of a popcorn bag from the movie theatre and have crinkled up paper that looks like popcorn sticking out of it. But...here's the cool thing. We have real popcorn to hand out in baggies for people to eat while they watch the movie later that night." Maia spaced out as she flung this amazing idea at me.

"WOW!" That was my reaction to both Maia's brilliant idea and Max's big mess I had to collect in a doggie bag. "I like that idea. But, wait. Last year I think they had a concession stand during the movie. All the money raised was to help keep the park clean and safe. I'm sure it's the same this year," I reminded her as I tied up the baggie.

"Oh, you're right. We don't want to get anyone mad if we hand out free stuff and then they don't make money for the park," Maia said and let out a deep breath of defeat.

We rounded the corner and headed back to Mrs. Henderson's. She was waiting for us on the porch. She waved to us as we got closer. Max lifted Maia off the ground as he started sprinting to greet Mrs. Henderson. Maia had to keep up if she wanted to save her arm from being torn from her body. Yep, she was right. No way Max was going to be part of our float. But he was a part of who we are...kind of.

Buster had his wet nose pressed against the window anxiously waiting for us. When he saw us walking up the drive he hopped around in a circle and barked. "He's such a cute spaz," Maia said.

"Only when he's behaving," I replied.

By the time we got the hide-away key and unlocked the door in the back of the house, Buster was already panting like he had run a marathon. "Goodness, someone is happy to see us or really, really needs to pee," I laughed.

I held him tight while Maia leashed him. Then it was only a matter of seconds before he did his routine of sniffing, circling, squatting, and kicking up grass. It was a hilarious scene. I'd make a video of it if I had a phone to take a video with. Soon, I hoped.

"Well, that was fast. Should we still walk him?" I said. I knew we should, but I was worried we were running out of time to build our parade float.

"Of course, we have to. I don't want to get fired. We haven't had any new customers since the puppies. We can't afford to lose any," Maia said, already making her way to the front of the house with Buster.

"Yea, yea I know. We just have so much planning to do. And actual float building, too," I groaned.

We started walking side by side with Buster leading the way. "What if we do something to help us get more business," Maia said. "Something to do with the pets."

"I was thinking that too."

"Not have them pull the float, but maybe make the float look like pets or...I don't know," I was starting to get discouraged as I said it aloud. It sounded better in my head.

"Maybe we get those huge parade balloons that look like characters and animals," Maia said.

"That would be amazing. But I bet they're expensive. And where would we even get one?" I crushed that idea. "Let's cross the street." I motioned to the truck that was blocking the sidewalk up ahead.

We jogged across the street and continued our walk. When we passed the truck, it had a huge picture of a wooden playset painted on the side. Some lucky little kid was getting a playset in his yard. Parts of it were sitting in front of the house. A swing was tossed on the lawn, a few large pieces of wood were leaning against a tree trunk, and the one thing that really caught my eye; the roof that goes over the platform that attaches to the slide.

LIGHTBULB.

"Why don't we build a red, white, and blue doghouse!?" I shouted.

"You scared the heck out of me," Maia responded and slapped my arm.

"Sorry, but look." I pointed across the street. "The top of that playset looks like a doghouse...sort of. It doesn't look like it is made out of much. Just wood nailed together. Can't be too hard, right?"

"Not too hard? Those people hired professionals to put it together for them." Maia looked at me with her eyes all bugging out of her head.

"Don't look at me like that."

"Sorry, but how are we supposed to build a doghouse big enough to be a float?" Maia asked.

"I can ask my dad to help. He has plenty of tools. We just need to get wood. Three sides and two more pieces that make a roof."

"OMG!"

"What? What?" I exclaimed.

"My dad told my mom that he wanted to tear out all the paneling in our attic and remodel it into an office," Maia explained.

"What is paneling?" I asked.

Buster barked at the playset workers that emerged from the back of the truck. "Shh, Buster," I said. "Keep going."

Maia tugged Buster along and his attention turned to a butterfly that fluttered around us. He jumped and tried catching it. We just watched. It was entertaining.

"Okay, so what is paneling, anyway?" I asked again.

"Just thin pieces of wood that has lines in it. It is all over the walls in our attic. It would be perfect to use. And free." Maia was excited about that last comment. So was I.

"Do you think he will let us use it?" I asked.

"I don't see why not. It's like recycling, right? He's a big recycler," Maia sounded hopeful.

Buster went to the bathroom again and we took him back home. We had some serious planning to do. More like serious pleading for help to do. Maia was put in charge of convincing her dad to let us use the paneling and I was going to persuade my dad to help us build the float. We rushed through the rest of our pet jobs with only one thing on our minds.

I sprawled out across my bed with a pad of paper and markers and brainstormed. I had my TV on, but I wasn't paying any attention to it. I drew a picture of a doghouse and showed it to my dad when he peeked his head into my room. *It's too much work to get done on short notice,* is what I expected him to say. But, to my surprise, he didn't. He said he would help build it if Maia's dad agreed to let us have the panels. Maia called the house around eight o'clock, which woke up Brownie and got my mom upset. If I had a cell phone, she could have texted me instead of calling the house phone that rings so loud it wakes up a two-year-old. Having to use the house phone is on my GRRR list.

Maia's dad was onboard. Our float was his motivation to begin the renovation project on the attic. All this good news kept me awake perfecting our design. I colored in the doghouse roof with stars and stripes. My brain was spinning out of control with ideas. Maybe one of the dog owners would let us walk one of the dogs in the parade wearing a patriotic bandana. I looked over at my closet and remembered something.

I leapt out of bed. Jammed in the corner of my closet was a pile of old stuffed animals. Buried on the bottom was the one I needed. I used to lay on it to watch TV when I was a kid. I held up Mr. Fluffy. I was six at the time and not very creative with names, but he was perfect. A jumbo stuffed dog. We could make him look like he is coming out of the doghouse. We can even dress him up in a cute t-shirt, I thought.

Shirts! We could have matching shirts to advertise our business.

Tuesday, June 29

First thing in the morning I asked my mom where we could have business shirts made. She reminded me that shirts would cost money. BOOM! There goes a small chunk of my cell phone money.

"You could always make them," my mom suggested.

"Mom, we want to look professional. Not some sloppy kid stuff."

"Don't roll your eyes," she snapped. "You can make them look nice with iron-on letters."

"Maybe." I shrugged at the idea.

"I even saw a bunch of patches you can use at the craft store. I'm positive I saw animals," my mom went on.

"How much is that gonna cost?" I moaned.

"I have coupons. Probably about ten dollars for each of you."

"Really!" I squealed.

This sounded like a legit plan I had to tell Maia about. MOTHERS! And their coupons!

I rushed out the door with a warmed-up egg and bacon sandwich from the freezer. It sounds disgusting, I know. But the biscuit that holds it all together is dipped in syrup before it's frozen and tastes amazing. I told Maia all about the shirts with a cheek stuffed with food.

"Try not to choke, please," Maia laughed at me. "You look like a squirrel."

"I can't help it. This is so good. So, what do you think?" I asked still chewing.

"I'm in. We just need to pick a cool color for our shirts," Maia said.

"Oh totally," I said. Then we high-fived.

Max was eager as ever when he saw us coming. Mrs. Henderson opened the screen door before Maia was close enough to take his leash. Bad Mrs. Henderson!

I almost choked on my bacon and egg biscuit sandwich. The three-legged monster raced down the steps. Drool sprayed through the air as he flashed his blood-thirsty fangs. I could hear panting as he leapt from the last step and with three large strides he lunged forward. I didn't even have time to run, or scream, because my mouth was full of sandwich. Max's paws collided with my chest with a force that knocked me to the ground. I was sprawled out and pinned down. I closed my eyes so he couldn't see the fear in my eyes. There was no avoiding his rotten breath. His nose was against mine and snot was dripping onto my face. I turned my head away. Big mistake; that left my neck wide open for his razor teeth to take the perfect bite. They'd sink deeply into my vein and I would be a goner. I've seen detective shows when they outline the dead body with tape. That's how I'd be remembered, as an outline on the sidewalk in front of Mrs. Henderson's house. I was going to be Hocking Hills' next, maybe only, crime scene.

I wedged my sandwichless-hand between me and Max just as I heard Maia yell, "No, no, no, Max. Get off Paige!"

She grabbed ahold of his collar, but he was relentless. He resisted her tugging and leaned forward with all his weight almost bringing Maia down on top of me. He stretched and pulled, claws digging into my shoulder until he finally reached my sandwich-holding hand. NO! He snatched the rest of my egg and bacon sandwich right out of it. I don't think he even stopped to enjoy its delicious syrupy flavor. He swallowed it in one gulp, then licked his chops.

16

He was now satisfied, and I was still alive. I should be happy about that, but I wasn't. Mrs. Henderson made her way down from the porch and hooked on the leash as Maia held Max. Then Maia held out her hand and helped me up. I tried to be brave, but when Mrs. Henderson said, "I'm so sorry, dear. Are you alright? He didn't hurt you, did he?" tears bubbled up in my eyes and then they popped.

"He is so mean!" I blurted.

I stormed off walking quickly down the street. "Paige, wait!" Maia called after me.

I didn't stop. I just wanted to be alone. Maia finally caught up to me at the corner where I had stopped to sulk. I didn't want to go home. My mom might tell me that I wasn't cut out for dog sitting, and I should quit. I didn't want to be treated like a baby on top of everything else. Or she would tell me to fulfill my responsibilities and get back to work. I didn't want to do that either. GRRR!

"Are you okay?" Maia asked as she came closer, making sure to keep Max on her other side.

"No. I'm so sick of him being so mean to me," I growled.

"He just wanted your sandwich," Maia said. "Here," she held out her hand, "these are from Mrs. Henderson. She feels awful."

I looked down at Maia's hand. She had a bag of cookies. They were chocolate chip, my favorite! I took them from her and was about to open them but saw Max eyeing them too.

"No, bad dog. Not for you." I stuck my tongue out at Max.

He licked his nose, but I think he was just sticking his tongue back at me.

"Are you going to walk with us or just go home?" Maia asked.

"If you keep him away from me, I'll come," I said and wiped my eyes.

"I promise," Maia said, and we started walking.

We walked slower than usual. I think Max knew he was in trouble and didn't even try to sprint ahead. I quietly opened the bag of cookies and nudged Maia with my arm. "You want one?" I asked. I was still hungry since meanie Max devoured half my food. I couldn't wait to sink my teeth into the gooey chocolate.

"No thank you," she whispered then gasped. "OMG, you're bleeding!" She covered her mouth with her hand.

"What?"

"Your elbow is all bloody." Maia pointed to it.

So, Max did draw blood after all. If only I could find a way to pay him back for what he's done. This wasn't the first time he has caused me agony and probably wouldn't be the last. I licked two of my fingers and tried to rub some of the blood off my elbow. It had already started to dry. But when I rubbed the cut it stung. GRRR!

Quince was typical Quince today. He waddled his way down the street and plopped down. But, today was hot and we didn't gripe. We sat down with him under a shaded area and took a break too. Poor Quince just sat there and panted with his tongue nearly hitting the cement. "Really wish we could get this dog to lose weight," I said as I pet his back.

"I don't think there is anything we can do. Even if we did invent the dog treadmill, do you really think we could get him on it?" Maia said with a laugh.

"Not a chance," I replied.

"Well, we definitely can't have Quince walk with us in the parade. He doesn't even really walk," Maia said.

"Max is out too," I quickly said.

"Well, duh! Maybe Quince can sit on the float," Maia said.

"No way. He weighs too much. I am not pulling him two miles. Not a chance," I said.

"Good point," Maia said as she picked a few blades of grass then blew them out of her hand.

"Sandy is a good dog once she gets the anxious jumpy-jumps out of her. Definitely not Buster. Way too fast. If he got loose, he would ruin the entire parade," I rambled.

"Maybe Lucy can do it. I can send a text and ask," Maia suggested.

"Good idea. Do it now so we can plan ahead."

After Maia sent the text, we waited a few minutes for a response. When we didn't get one, I said, "We better get this big butt movin'. Come on Quince, we gotta go home." I nudged him and he slowly made his way up to his paws, which made him only a few more inches off the ground. "Short and fat. Poor guy." I laughed at my own joke.

After we scooted Quince through the doggy door, we went to Ryan Too-Cutie Shootie's house. I let Maia feed the fish while I watched them swim around. Okay, I pretended to watch them swim. Ryan's picture that was on the table near the fish tank was blurry through the glass and water, but I could still see it. I wondered if he was riding The Scorpion, while we were busy working, feeding *his* fish. Hope he wasn't squeezing anyone else's hand, I thought.

"All done. Stop staring at Ryan and let's go," Maia said.

"I wasn't!" My face was chili pepper hot.

I don't even remember walking Sandy and Buster. We were just too busy talking about our float that it all went so fast. Too fast. We were running out of time.

Maia called after dinner and told me that her dad started tearing out the paneling in the attic. There were enough pieces for us to get started.

"I'll walk down with Brian's wagon to get the wood," I told Maia before I hung up.

"Can I come help?" my little sister Sarah asked.

"There's nothing for you to help with," I told her.

"Yes, there is. Mom! Paige is being mean. I just want to pull the wagon." Sarah stomped her foot.

"You can help Dad while he builds the doghouse, okay?" I said.

Sarah beamed at the idea. "Can I have a pet shirt too and walk in the parade with you?"

"We can dress you up like a dog and you can shake your butt and wag your tail." I smiled imagining how funny she would look.

"Really? Thanks Paige!" Sarah's smile almost looked terrifying.

"UM, no! That is just ridiculous. I was only kidding," I said.

"You are so mean. I wanna be a dog in the parade," Sarah whined.

"Well you are halfway there," I laughed.

"What does that mean?" Sarah snarled.

I just laughed.

"What does that mean, Paige? That I'm a dog?" Sarah yelled. She may have been close to crying but I was too busy laughing to know for sure.

Wednesday, June 30

Hot and sweaty would be an understatement for the day on the job. But there was no time for water fights or sprinklers. We had work to do. Parade float work. Plus, we had a new sitting job!

When I met Maia in the morning the first thing she said was, "We have another job."

"Awesome. Who? What is it, a dog?"

"A rabbit," Maia said excitedly.

"Oh wow! I never really thought about someone having a rabbit," I said.

"His name is Gunther. They just got him from the pet store like two weeks ago, but now they are going to visit family for a week and don't want to travel with a rabbit," Maia said.

"Perfect. How much will they pay us?" I asked eagerly.

"She said she would pay us forty dollars, which I said was fine since we don't have to be there long. We just have to feed it then let it hop around the kitchen to get some exercise," Maia explained.

"When do we go meet them?"

"They are leaving today, so we have to go right after we walk Max. They got our names from the Smiths. I got a text back. Lucy and the puppies are going camping for the weekend with the Smiths so she can't be in the parade with us, but asked if she could pass our name along to her neighbor who was in desperate need of a pet sitter. I said, 'of course, of course'," Maia rambled.

"Rabbits are so cute. Can't wait," I squealed.

"So, do we find out if Sandy can walk in the parade?" I asked.

"She's probably our next best option," Maia said.

After a typical Max morning and his mess was locked up in a baggie, we hurried over to meet Gunther.

He's a pretty rabbit, if a boy rabbit doesn't mind being called pretty. His brown hair is super fluffy. His little nose twitched at us through his cage as if he were saying hello.

"Are you girls okay with handling him? Like lifting him in and out of the cage?" Anna (she said we could call her Anna and not Mrs. Arnold) said.

"Sure," Maia said. Of course, she was sure.

Anna unlocked the cage. She lifted the rabbit out and handed him to Maia. "Just set him down in the kitchen to have some freedom for a little bit when you come to feed him. I'll have our old baby gate up so he can't run throughout the house." She waved us over to the kitchen and Maia set Gunther on the floor.

"Food is there on the floor. There is a bag of celery and lettuce leaves in the refrigerator. A piece of each is fine. The pet store told us to make sure you put the hay at one end of the cage away from his litter box, so he won't poop in his food," Anna explained.

Maia and I looked at each other and smiled a squeamish smile. That would be totally nasty, I thought.

"How long should we let him hop around?" I asked.

"As long as you have the time. Fifteen minutes maybe. Longer if you aren't busy," Anna said.

Not busy? She obviously doesn't know we have a float to finish.

"Water, Mom. Remember the water," a little voice said.

I turned around and a little girl who looked about Sarah's age was standing behind us.

"This is Abby. Gunther was her birthday present," Anna said.

"Hi," Maia and I both said.

"Wow, that's a cool birthday present," I added.

"He's my favorite. Are you going to take care of him?" Abby asked.

"Yep. We will take good care of Gunther," Maia said.

"Cool. Thank you. Don't forget to give him water," Abby said. She's a lot nicer than Sarah.

"Right," Anna said. "There is a little water bottle. Just make sure its full when you leave. Come on, I will show you how to detach it."

Maia let me scoop up Gunther and she held the cage door open. He was so soft and cuddly. Then Anna gave us a house key and said she would get it back when the family returned. This was going to be an easy-peasy sitting job. The best kind.

Waiting for my dad to get home was almost as torturous as having to play with Sarah. But we had shirts to make and details to figure out in the meantime.

My mom took us to the store to buy shirts and iron-on patches. We decided on blue shirts. Blue is a cheery color. Cat and dog patches were the only ones we saw that we could use. They had lizards, birds, and dinosaurs, but those made no sense! Maybe a bird, but they creep me out so I didn't want to advertise that we would take care of them.

When the cashier hit the total button on the register it flashed $52.40. OMG! What? My eyes bugged out of my head. That was a lot of my cell phone fund. My mom gave the cashier her coupon and the total dropped to $20.70. Much better! Maia and I had to part with ten dollars and thirty-five cents each. Hopefully, getting more customers would make it worthwhile.

Of course, Sarah begged and cried for us to make her a shirt as well. She was ruining our concentration.

"We only have enough letters for one word. Go get an old t-shirt," I told her. When she returned from her bedroom with a bright yellow shirt, I arranged the letters across the front of it—PEST.

"Hey, that doesn't spell pets. Mom! Paige is making me a shirt that says pest. I am not a pest."

I laughed until my mom glared at me. "The least you can do is make your sister a shirt since your dad is helping you out with this project," she said.

I had a feeling she wasn't giving me a choice. GRRR!

We worked in the garage; measuring, cutting, and hammering. My dad did most of the work, but he did let us help. Maia almost hammered her thumb, which was sort of funny. Surprisingly, it didn't take long to get the frame built. My dad used his nail gun to attach some two-by-four pieces of wood to the bottom so it would stand up and not fall over. It fit perfectly inside the wagon.

Things were going perfectly...until I tripped and knocked over a box of nails. "Paige," my dad huffed.

"Sorry, it was an accident," I huffed back.

They were scattered all over. "I'll help you pick them up," Maia said.

"Thank you, Maia," my dad said.

We crawled around on the ground picking up nails until Maia got a text.

"It's my mom. I gotta get home," she said.

Maia left and my mind kept working. "Do you have paint I can use?" I asked my dad.

"I wanna paint," Sarah said as she appeared from nowhere.

"No chance," I snapped.

She stuck her tongue out at me. I had the same childish response.

"I have some leftover paint—white and maybe some blue—from when we redid Brian's bedroom. No red. But, no painting tonight. It's getting late. You'll have to start that tomorrow."

Great. Where was I going to get red paint on such short notice? More cell phone money.

Thursday, July 1

When Maia and I went to pick up Max for his walk, he was sitting on the porch with Mrs. Henderson. She was waiting with more cookies. She still felt really bad about Max's behavior the other day.

"Mrs. Henderson, you don't have to keep giving me cookies," I said. But I didn't hesitate to take them. One last batch wouldn't hurt. As we started walking, a drop of water bounced off my forehead. I looked up and saw a white canvas streaked with large gray strokes.

"It's starting to rain," I said.

"I didn't even notice the clouds," Maia said.

"Maybe it'll just drizzle. We better hurry just in case though." I gave Maia a pleading look.

"Are you up for a jog?" she asked.

"What?"

"Come on Max, you wanna run?" Maia said in her sweet, excited dog whisperer voice and started galloping.

29

"Oh no, what did you do, Maia?" I panicked and laughed at the same time.

Max quickly caught on. Once he picked up momentum, he was pulling Maia along instead of the other way around.

I couldn't believe this was Maia's brilliant idea to hurry jobs along. I stood there shaking my head in disbelief, then I had to sprint to catch up. We made it halfway down the block before Maia wanted to stop. "Max! Slow down!" she yelled.

"This was your idea," I laughed. I was nearly out of breath as well though.

Max being Max, didn't listen, until he spotted a squirrel. He barked up a tree trunk.

"No, Max, we can't get the squirrel, he is too high even for Super Max," Maia said in her dog whisperer voice.

He looked back at Maia. "No Max, come on. We have treats." She looked at me and asked, "We have treats, right?"

I patted my pocket to make sure they were there. "Yes, Max, we have your treats if you're a good boy," I said, not quite as sweetly as Maia.

Maia pulled his leash and we jogged some more. A few wet spots appeared on the cement in front of us, but no thunder or lightning, just a quick summer sprinkle. All that running for nothing. Although it did tire out Max enough that he sat nicely as he waited for his treat instead of trying to gobble it up along with my hand like he normally does.

Next stop was Gunther.

"Hi Gunther. You wanna come out and play?" I said softly.

"Look who has a soft spot for rabbits," Maia joked.

"Well I know he won't attack me like mean 'ol Max," I argued. Then I turned my attention back to Gunther as I unlocked the cage. "Whatcha doing, silly rabbit? Why is all your hay piled up like that?" I turned to Maia, "Should we put new stuff down? He has it all jammed together in the corner."

"Well, let's just flatten that back out. He might just be getting used to his new home," Maia said.

"Good point."

I scooped up Gunther and he wriggled around so much I almost dropped him. "Hey, hey, it's okay. You're just going to go play," I said and handed him over to Maia, who cradled him like a baby. She sure does have the animal instinct.

"You sure are a big fluffy thing, aren't you, Gunther?" Maia went all pet whisperer on me.

The easy-peasy rabbit job was done in no time at all. I flattened out Gunther's hay and filled the water bottle while Maia rolled up the newspaper covered in rabbit droppings and got him some veggies. Gunther was back in his cage after fifteen minutes.

Quince walked at an extra-slow pace today. He almost looked as if he was limping. His waddle was a little crooked.

"Does he seem okay to you?" I asked Maia.

"Maybe he's just fatter on one said than the other," Maia joked.

"Ha, funny." I bent down and pet Quince along his back. Then I rubbed his chest area. When I touched the area where his stubby leg meets his body (a dog shoulder?), it sounded like Quince cried.

"Did you hear that?" I looked up at Maia.

"No. Touch him again," Maia said.

"I don't want to hurt him."

"Just be gentle," Maia said.

I softly rubbed the same spot on Quince's leg and he definitely whimpered. "You poor guy. I think we should take you home," I said looking into Quince's sad eyes and rubbing his ears.

"Now look who's the dog whisperer," Maia smiled.

"Well, he's hurt. And he's never done anything rude to me like you know who," I protested.

"Come on Paige the softy. Let's get Quince home." Maia started walking.

"Wait, let's go slow," I said.

"Paige, that is the only speed Quince knows."

Maia was right, but I still said, "I mean slower."

We walked and Quince limped at a snail's pace. He stopped to rest and I patiently waited...until I spotted that purple bike coming down the road. I turned my attention to Quince, "Come on buddy, just a little farther, I know you can do it." I looked back up and the bike carrying know-it-all Ashley was almost to us.

"Can't we just carry him from here?" I nudged Maia.

"We did that once before and almost hurt ourselves," Maia reminded me.

"But here comes...oh, hi Ashley." I waved and looked back down at Quince.

"Having a problem or something?" Ashley asked.

"Nothing we can't handle," Maia said.

"Are you sure about that? Looks like your pooch is struggling. Do you need me to get the cart I'm using for my July Fourth float? It's huge, that dog will totally fit."

"His name is Quince," I snapped.

Ashley flipped her hair. "Yeah, I knew that. Sorry. So, like do you want my help or not?"

"No thank you," Maia said politely.

"I was asking Paige. She's the one holding the leash," Ashley snarled.

I wanted to knock her off her bike. How dare she talk to Maia that way. "*We* do not need your help, Ashley," I said through my teeth so I wouldn't scream and upset poor Quince.

"Okay, I was just trying to be legit friendly."

"Um, don't you have your float to work on?" I asked.

"Oh, I am so totally done with it. I texted Ryan last night and he said he was going to be home just in time for the parade. He is going to look great on my float. Don't ya think?" Ashley smiled.

"No, actually I don't think he will," I snapped.

Breathe Paige! BREATHE! That's all I could tell myself or I would have exploded with anger.

"What exactly is your float, Ashley?" Maia asked.

"Wouldn't you like to know," Ashley responded.

"Um, yea, that's why she asked it, duh," I huffed.

"Well, I'm not giving any hints. I wouldn't want you to steal my idea."

"Ours is done too, we don't need your ideas," I growled.

Quince whimpered. I must have unknowingly tugged on his leash out of frustration. "Oh, you poor Quince. Let's get you home," I said in my new dog whisperer voice.

"Here comes a car, don't get hit, Ashley," Maia said.

"Yea, we wouldn't want anything bad to happen to you," I said and whipped my hair over my shoulder the Ashley way. "Come on Maia, let's get Quince home."

"I'll make sure to tell Ryan you don't think he'll look good in the parade," Ashley shouted over her shoulder as she started peddling.

"I didn't say that!" I yelled. My hands were curled up in fists. I could feel my nails dig into the palms of my hands. GRRR!

"How are you so calm around her?" I asked Maia.

"My mom said to just ignore her attitude and when she sees it doesn't bother us, she'll stop."

"Not sure that'll work. I think her whole family has a bad attitude," I said.

"Just give it time. She'll realize she's only hurting herself."

"Your mom tell you that, too?" I said.

"Yep." Maia shrugged.

MOTHERS! Let's hope she's right.

Quince hesitated to go into the doggy door, and I didn't want to shove him through. I waited and waited, but he just sat there staring at me.

"Why don't you go feed the fish and I'll make sure he goes in the house. It might rain more, and I don't want him out here hurt," I told Maia.

"Are you sure? I can stay so you can gawk at Ryan's pic," Maia said.

"I don't gawk. And I don't want to see him, especially if he is really Ashley's float partner. How nasty is that?" I cringed.

"She's lying," Maia said.

"How do you know? It's not like I can call or text him to ask. I don't know his number. I don't even have a cell phone, remember?"

My GRRR list was getting longer and longer by the day.

"Do you want me to text him?" Maia asked.

"OMG, no!" I shook my head. "That would be so weird. No way. Besides, we don't know his number," I said.

"I'm sure someone from school has it," Maia said.

"Like Cory. Do you have Cory's number? Have you been talking to Cory?" I teased.

"Actually, no." Maia sounded disappointed.

"Oh." I was disappointed for the both of us.

Maia left and I sat with Quince. He placed his head in my lap and I rubbed his ears. His head was making my leg fall asleep. I couldn't get up if I wanted to. (I didn't want to.) A few more raindrops fell, but I could see blue skies peeking around the clouds, so I wasn't worried. We just sat. Then out of nowhere Quince sat up and waddled through the doggy dog. I was actually curious to see why he had gone in so abruptly, so I stuck my head through the rubber flap. Just as I suspected, he was hungry. His bowl was right next to the doggy door. He sniffed his food and looked back at me.

"Good boy, Quince," I said as I tried to get my head out of the door.

OH NO! How come it fit in but not out? I could feel that panicky feeling rolling up from my stomach. Just try again, I said to myself. I scooted back and pulled my head towards the door. The door was just too small. I turned my head from side to side. I still couldn't get out. My ears...were my ears too big? I don't think I have big ears, but maybe for a doggy door I do. Quince's big butt can fit through the door, but my ears can't? No, it was my shoulder. I was farther in than I thought. What was I going to do now? My knees began to hurt as they pressed into the cement patio.

"Please hurry back, Maia," I pleaded.

Quince waddled two steps away from his food dish and sat down so we were face to face. I'm all for affection, but his wet dog tongue sliding across my face was a bit much.

"Gross, Quince. No licking," I tried to wipe my cheek on the top of my shoulder. "This is so embarrassing, Quince. You have no idea. Okay, well you walk around looking like that every day, so maybe you do. But still." I wasn't sure why I was talking. I didn't know what else to do.

I wiggled and pulled once more, but still my enormous head wouldn't come out. Then I heard a laugh.

"OMG. I have to take a picture of this." Maia's voice was muffled, but I knew it was her. Thank goodness it was only her.

"No. No pictures!" I shouted.

That must have startled Quince. He barked at me and I flinched, hitting my neck on the frame of the doggy door. "OUCH!" I shouted again.

"What are you doing?" Maia said.

"I'm stuck. Please get me out," I begged.

"Twist your shoulders to the left and then pull back," Maia said.

I did what she told me and my shoulder broke free.

"My head is still stuck." I was close to tears.

"It's your ponytail. It's too high. Lift your hand and take out the ponytail holder," Maia instructed.

"I can't reach the top of my head," I mumbled.

"Okay. Okay."

There was silence. Then more silence.

"Are you there?" I said.

"I'm thinking," Maia responded.

Click.

"What was that?" I asked.

"Nothing."

"You took a picture of me, didn't you?" I yelled.

"Maybe. I thought you might want to see how funny this is," Maia laughed.

"It's not funny. Get me out," I grumbled.

"I'll loosen your hair out of the ponytail from back here until it falls completely out," Maia said.

"I don't care what you try. Just no more pictures," I said.

Maia wedged her hand under the rubber flap that was resting on the top of my back.

"OUCH!" I shouted.

"Sorry, sorry," Maia said as she ruffled my hair trying to shake the hairs out of the ponytail that was planted tight and high on the top of my head. I could feel it fall to my neck. Slowly all the hair started to come free from my ponytail. I shook my head back and forth. Quince, who was still an inch from my face, shook his head too. I couldn't help but laugh. Then the blue scrunchie fell to the floor. Quince sniffed it.

"No, no Quince. That's not yours," I said.

"Try to get out now," Maia instructed.

I slowly scooted my legs and hands back. Then I closed my eyes. I have no idea why I closed my eyes. It just felt like a more powerful thing to do. I sucked my cheeks in and eased my head out of the doggy door. It was a miracle. It fit. My head was free! BFF to the rescue AGAIN!

"OMG! I can't believe I was stuck in there. That was the worst thing ever," I said.

"More like funniest," Maia said with a smile.

"Stop."

"Your scrunchie," Maia reminded me.

"Oh yea." I stuck my hand into the doggy door and felt for my scrunchie. It felt a little wet from Quince's spit, but I wasn't going to scold him. He was having a bad day as it was.

"How is he?" Maia asked.

"He was total chillax. Just laid his head on my lap. But then he got hungry and bolted in to eat."

"Bolted?" Maia said shockingly.

"Okay, not bolted. It's Quince. He just stood up out of nowhere and went in to eat. He was still limping though. Maybe you should send a text to Mandi, so she know he's hurt," I suggested.

"Good idea," Maia said and pulled her phone from her pocket.

"Make sure she knows we didn't do anything to him," I said kind of nervous.

"I don't think she will think that." Maia started typing.

The freedom to send messages to whomever you wish whenever you wish. One day soon, I hoped.

When we got home from our sitting jobs we had much to do. Maia brought over the red paint her mom bought for us and we got started painting right away. My stars were horribly uneven. We ended up painting over them and making a stencil out of a piece of cardboard. Then they were perfect.

We stood back and looked at our large doghouse. "Looks pretty good," Maia said.

"I know, right? It's a legit float. Way better than Ashley's," I said. We high-fived.

Friday, July 2

As I went out the garage door to go meet Maia in the morning, I poked the roof of our doghouse float. It was dry. I was beyond excited. Everything was falling into place. Know-it-all Ashley is going to be so jealous, I thought. Unless of course, she has some really huge over-the-top Ashley float. She probably didn't even do the work and had a professional carpenter do it for her. I growled a loud GRRR and left.

I met Maia at the corner and we walked down Maplewood Drive together as usual. Maia was still eating her granola bar. In between bites she said, "No Quince today."

"What? Why?" I asked.

"Mandi called after she got home from work," Maia said. "She said he never ate and is still limping."

"But he went right over to his food bowl and ate," I said then paused. "Wait. He didn't actually eat. He just sort of sniffed it and then he came over to lick my face. You didn't tell her I got stuck, did you?"

"No, I forgot about that part," Maia laughed. "And she asked if he went to the bathroom when we took him for a walk."

"He did, didn't he?"

"I thought he did, but she said he went in the house, which isn't like him," Maia trailed off.

"So, why aren't we going over there today?" I asked.

"She is taking him to the vet. So, Mandi will just take care of him for the day, I guess," Maia shrugged.

"Poor Quince. I hope he gets better soon," I said with a forced smile.

"Me too, but it does give us some extra time to get ready for the parade," Maia said.

"True. The float totally needs another coat on the red and white stripes. We'll do that after we finally get done with Buster and Sandy," I said.

"And Gunther," Maia remembered.

"How could I forget Gunther, the cutest rabbit ever!" I said.

Max was more cooperative today than usual. He simply licked my hand as he walked by and pretty much ignored me until it was time for his treats. It almost made me change my opinion of him. ALMOST! He was definitely still on my GRRR list, just not as high up today. Sandy was jumpy, but controllable. We played fetch with her for a few minutes in the back yard before we took her on a walk. That seemed to calm her down.

When we unlocked the door to take care of Buster, I looked over at Maia and her face was expressing what I was thinking. It was shriveled with disgust.

"What in the world is that nasty smell?" I said.

"OMG, I have no idea." Maia hid her nose in the top of her shirt.

"Did you step in dog poop?" I mumbled through my hand that was covering my mouth and pinching my nose at the same time.

"No!" Maia said but checked her shoes anyway. "Did you?"

"I think I would know if..." I lifted my left foot. All clear, but when I lifted my right foot, I quickly put it down so I wouldn't have to look right at it. It was there. Stuck into the creases on the bottom of my sandal.

"Paige! Don't step on the floor with it on your shoe," Maia screeched. I know she wasn't yelling at me, but it sure felt like it.

"I didn't mean to!" I shrieked. "How the heck did I step in it and not know?"

"I don't know, but you have to wash it off. It smells so bad." Maia buried her face again in her shirt.

Buster was frantically circling us, smelling my feet. He knew some other dog's mess was in his house. ICK!

"I'll take Buster out back." Maia picked him up. "You hose off."

"I got it on the floor. Can you get me some paper towels first?" I pleaded.

"He needs to go out or he'll make a mess in here too," Maia said.

"Fine."

I took off my sandal and found some paper towels and cleaner in a spray bottle. I quickly wiped up the mess and wadded up the paper towels. So gross!

I tossed them in the outside garbage can and stepped through the grass very carefully, like I was trying to avoid a booby trap. I found the hose on the side of the house. I could hear Maia having more fun than me while she played with Buster. Why did everything seem to happen to me? GRRR! I did everything I could not to gag as I sprayed water on my sandal, flinging dog poop into the air. How was I ever going to wear these sandals again?

"What are you doing?" an irritating voice said.

I didn't want to look up. I knew who it was. Why did she always appear at the worst moments? I continued to spray my sandal pretending I didn't hear Ashley.

"Did you step in dog poop?" Her voice seemed to be closer.

"No! It was mud." I had to lie. Who knows who she'd tell? Probably Ryan. "Are you following us? How did you even know I was here?" I asked.

"I was just heading up to the Gas & Go and saw you struggling."

"No one said I was struggling, Ashley," I groaned. "You can go to Gas & Go now."

"Are you and Maia really going to be done with your float on time for the parade? I wouldn't want you to miss it," Ashley said.

"So nice of you," I said. I doubt she saw me roll my eyes. I was too busy examining my shoe, which I would rather be doing than talking to Ashley.

"Okay, well, I'm always available to help out if you need me," Ashley said as she walked her bike back to the street.

She always sounds so sweet when she says stuff like that, but I know she has an ulterior motive. She always does. I didn't look up and acknowledge her until she said, "Ryan is going to love hearing this story."

GRRR! She's lucky I can't throw that far because I might've whipped my sandal at her.

Instead, I rubbed the bottom of my sandal against the grass and rewashed it with the hose. Maia finished playing with Buster just as I turned the faucet nozzle off.

"Who were you talking to?" Maia asked as I was sliding on my sandal. It was wet and squishy.

"Ashley. She did most of the talking of course. She said she is going to tell Ryan I stepped in dog poop. How dare she?" My teeth were clenched tight as I spoke.

"She is just trying to get you mad. Ignore her," Maia said as we started walking.

"But I don't want him to know."

"Let's just focus on the float and get back at her by winning," Maia said.

"Yea, we need a way to get more votes," I said. Buster barked. "See, he agrees."

"He barks at butterflies," Maia laughed.

"We can give out dog treats," I said.

"Other floats tossed out candy last year. We can do that too," Maia said.

"True. Okay. Let's add that to the list."

"Candy for kids and treats for dogs. Perfect for our theme," Maia said.

Buster barked again.

"Sorry Buster, no treats right now," I said.

"After we get the float painted, we can go to the store," Maia said.

"I'll ask my mom, but she might not want to drag Brownie to the store," I said.

"What if we babysit?" Maia said.

"Not a chance. I dealt with enough poop today and Brownie is a poop machine," I said.

Maia laughed.

"Hopefully it won't cost too much to buy both candy and dog treats," I said.

Buster barked again.

"Still no, Buster," I said.

"Well, we are running out of time. We only have today and tomorrow to get to the store," Maia said.

"Buster get moving buddy. We've got lots to do," I said.

Sandy was a breeze today, so we ended up at Gunther's a few minutes early. When we got to the house, we noticed that all the hay in his cage was piled up again in one corner.

"What is your deal fuzzy little dude?" I said as I lifted him from the cage.

He leapt from my arms as I sat him in the kitchen. He just looked up at me twitching his nose.

Maia reached into the cage with a celery stick to smooth out the hay again. Then we left him some veggies, a scoop of rabbit food, and water. He only got a few snuggles from us today because the float was priority number one until the parade was over.

I went inside with Maia to feed the fish. I was not about to wait outside and risk Ashley cruising by on her bike again. I wondered why she didn't have anything better to do all summer. Get a hobby, I thought.

Maia and I looked at each other, our eyes bulging out of our heads. Something was wrong. Terribly wrong. We could barely see the fish. It was like someone scooped up the dirtiest, scum-filled pond water and dumped it into the tank. ICK!

"OMG! What's the deal?" I asked Maia, not expecting her to have an answer. "Did you overfeed them yesterday?"

"I think I know better. That's your thing, remember?"

I gave Maia a sideways look and said, "that was an accident."

"There has to be another reason," Maia said.

"This is horrible. We have to get them out of there. What if they die?" My scratchy panic voice was rising.

"I can text Mrs. Shootie," Maia said.

"NO! Not yet. I mean, we don't want Ryan's mom to think we messed up. I think we should try to change the water, shouldn't we?" I could feel my forehead wrinkle in deep thought. Thoughts about Ryan hating us if we killed his family's fish.

"No way. Changing the water the wrong way will definitely kill the fish. It's gotta be done at the right temperature and with the right chemicals, I think," Maia said.

"Well, should I still feed them?" I picked up the bottle of fish food but made no attempt to feed them.

"Definitely," Maia said as she peeked around the back of the fish tank.

"What are you doing?" I asked. "Don't touch anything."

My eyes caught a glimpse of Ryan's framed picture. He was smiling. *Heart pounding.* He won't be smiling if we kill his fish. Or even talk to us again.

"You see anything?" I said.

"Not sure what I am looking for," Maia mumbled.

"Hey!" I blurted.

I startled Maia and she banged her head on the wooden stand the tank sat on. "Ouch!"

"OMG, are you okay?" I said giggling.

"Not really. What did you do that for?"

"Look. There aren't any bubbles. There used to be bubbles going up the side of the tank." I pointed to the side where I remembered seeing little bubbles float to the surface. "I didn't notice at first because the water is so dirty."

"The filter must be broken," Maia said.

"Are you kidding? We can't replace the filter. That is like lots of money for a tank like this."

I didn't mean to complain, but come on, we cannot afford to fix fish tanks for people. This was not part of the job description. I was starting to freak out. "I say we rescue the fish and put them in a bowl."

"Or," Maia said holding up a cord, "we plug the filter back in."

"Are you sure that's what it goes to?" I said half hopeful.

Maia followed the path of the cord up and, what do you know...it went to the filter. "Yep."

"Dude, plug it in. How did it get unplugged, anyway?"

"How am I supposed to know?" Maia said.

"Maybe our old-friend, the ghost cat, Wilma, wandered over here to the Shootie's," I laughed.

"Because that makes sense," Maia laughed at me.

"What? It could happen."

Maia plugged in the filter and we heard it switch on. I was never so happy to see little bubbles in all my life. We saved Ryan's fish. We were heroes if you ask me. Behind the tank Maia pulled out a small box filled with little yellow bottles, a fish net, and a broken, fake fish tank plant. "What are you doing with that stuff? We've done enough."

"I am just looking to see what it all is," Maia said lifting bottles and reading them. "Here." She stretched her arm up to me holding a yellow bottle. "Put two squirts of this in the water. It will kill the bacteria," she said.

"How do you know?" I said, slowly removing the cap as I waited for an answer.

"Um. It says right on the bottle."

"Oh." I felt sort of stupid. I held the bottle over the tank and gave it two squeezes. The drops hit the water and dispersed in an instant. "How will we know if it works?"

"We'll have to come back, I guess," Maia said, replacing the box behind the tank.

"That could have been a disaster," she said as she stood.

"Dude, no kidding," I said as I put the fish food away. I looked over at Ryan, he was still happily smiling, thanks to us.

"Should we just wait awhile to see if it works so we don't have to come back?" I asked.

"No. Let's just come back."

I wouldn't mind hanging out, but Maia was right, we couldn't waste any time. "Yeah, the float needs more paint. We can come back later today," I said.

My mom made us sandwiches for lunch and forced us to have a picnic with Sarah while she put Brian in the tub. Apparently, he made a mess with his lunch.

"This is the best picnic ever," Sarah said. "We should do this every day."

"Not a chance," I grumbled as I took my last bite. It was a beautiful day to just sit in the grass and daydream, if you're into that sort of thing.

"Okay, Sarah, we have work to do, so you have to go play," I said.

"Come on. Can't we chalk," Sarah whined.

"Maybe later," I said.

"Can I help you paint?" Sarah was acting like Ashley, who doesn't know when to stop.

"Probably not. It needs to be perfect," I said.

"Maybe it would go faster," Maia said.

I gave Maia an *are you kidding me* look.

"What? It's true. We still need to go buy candy and dog treats, and make a poster, and I'm sure there is something I'm forgetting," Maia rambled on.

I took a deep breath in and blew it out hard enough to hear it. "Fine, whatever. But you have to be careful and do it perfectly."

"YAY!" Sarah jumped up.

My gut was telling me this was going to be a mistake.

Things started out great. We each took a spot to work on so we weren't bumping into each other. We let Sarah paint the base of the doghouse while Maia and I added the second layer of paint to the stars and stripes on the roof. It was looking great! We rolled the float on the wagon out into the sun so the paint would dry faster, then treated ourselves to popsicles for all our hard work. While Maia and I sat on the front step of the house cooling off and chatting, we realized how quiet it had gotten. Sarah was nowhere to be seen, which is usually a good thing. It's almost always a good thing. Except this time. I looked over at the doghouse and saw Sarah in a cloud of glitter. Red and silver glitter was floating through the air. It looked like a unicorn exploded over our doghouse.

"NO! What are you doing?" I screamed at the top of my lungs.

"O...M...G." Maia was so stunned she said it slowly.

I ran over to Sarah and yanked the bottle of glitter from her hand. There was an empty bottle already lying on the ground. She had poured two entire bottles of glitter on the roof.

"You are such a brat! Why would you ruin our float? We didn't want glitter on it!" I growled. I literally growled. GRRR!

"Sarah, do you realize we'll have to repaint the entire doghouse?" Maia said in her dog whisperer voice.

"We are not babies; we do not want a glittery doghouse. Go away and leave us alone!" I yelled.

My mom appeared with her hands spread out like she was carrying a tray of food, but she wasn't holding anything. "What in the world is going on out here?" She demanded to know.

"Sarah ruined our float. Look what she did!" I huffed.

My mom saw the empty glitter bottles and the glitter that was spread all over the driveway. "Sarah go wash your hands and go up to your room please," my mom said calmly.

"But, Mom, I was only trying to help." Sarah started crying.

"Why are you the one crying? This isn't your ruined float," I snapped.

Sarah stomped away.

"Paige, enough. It can be fixed," my mom said.

"No, it can't!" I hollered back.

"Maia, would you mind giving us some time to cool off?"

"Sure," Maia said. "I'll call you later, Paige." Then she left. Poof, just like that, I was standing there alone. My mom made the only person on my side leave. How dare she? GRRR!

"Look, parade floats are more fun when they are loud and colorful and stand out. That's what they should look like. The glitter does just that. Look how shiny it is. Everyone will notice it for sure," my mom rambled.

She leaned her face close to the doghouse roof and blew on it. "What in the world are you doing?" I asked, almost embarrassed for her.

"Just seeing how much is actually stuck to the paint. If we brush off the excess glitter that didn't stick, it will be the perfect amount to give it the pop it needs without being clumpy and ruined," my mom said. "Get the broom and we'll brush some of it off."

I was reluctant to even consider this idea, but I gave in anyway. I handed my mom the broom from the garage and stood back as she gently grazed it across the doghouse. My stomach was in knots. What if she smeared all the paint? I wasn't sure I would have nice words about it. Glitter swirled and danced in the air before it floated to the ground.

When my mom was done dusting, she stood next to me. "See, look how amazing that looks," she said.

I didn't want to admit she was right. It had the perfect shine, and it really did look like a parade float now. MOTHERS!

"I'm still mad at Sarah," I mumbled. "She had no right to do that without asking."

"I know, I know. But I'm sure you can forgive her this time," my mom said giving my shoulder a half-hug.

Right before dinner I ran down the street to Maia's so we could check on the fish.

"How's the float disaster?" Maia asked immediately.

"Actually, it looks cool. It shimmers like a parade float should after we brushed some of it off. But, don't tell Sarah I said that."

"Trust me, I won't," Maia laughed.

We held our breathes as we entered the Shootie's house; not because it smelled like yucky fish tank funk, but we were nervous of what we would find.

"Oh my goodness. I can't believe it! Maia you saved the fish. You're a hero."

"Yes, yes, I am," Maia said smiling.

"Look. We can see the fish now. And there is only like one green icky thing floating around now. Ryan won't have to hate us." I was so happy.

"Totally. Okay, let's go. We still need to buy candy and dog treats. My mom said she'll drive us to the store," Maia said.

I never felt so relieved. The fish weren't dead, the float looked great, and the parade was only the day after tomorrow, which means, maybe, just maybe, Ryan Too-Cutie Shootie would be back in town.

Saturday, July 3

BANG, BANG, BANG, BANG! A pounding on the front door startled me. I was curled up on the couch attempting to get a jump start on my summer reading. I know July is a little late to start, but we've been so busy and this morning we didn't have any jobs. Not even Max. That is like a mini vacation. I had planned to paint my nails; my thumbs blue and alternating red and white for my other fingers. Very patriotic, I thought. But my mom nagged and nagged until I creased the first page in my book.

60

"I didn't spend a half hour in the library while your brother fussed for you NOT to read that book." That's the mini lecture my mom gave me.

I had actually gotten sucked into the story and nearly fell off the couch when someone banged on the door. GRRR!

"Paige, Maia is here," my mom called.

Okay, well, just let her in. I don't have to get up for Maia, I thought. But, after a minute she never strolled into the room, so I tossed the book on the floor and got up.

"Paige!" my mom called again.

"Coming!" I shouted back.

I walked down the hall leading to the front door and Maia was standing there slouched over. Her shoulders were curled in and her head was hanging low. Then she looked up at me with red, swollen eyes. Had she been crying?

"OMG! What happened? Is the float okay? Did something happen to the float? We don't have time to fix it." I spazzed out.

"No," Maia sniffled. "It's not the float. It's in your garage, remember?"

"Why are you crying then? Is it the fish? Holy cow, are the fish dead?" I couldn't stop my panicky voice.

61

"No, Paige. It's Quince." Maia sucked in a deep breath.

"What about him?"

"Mandi called. Quince…" Maia's voice got lost in a spit bubble in her throat. "Quince died."

"Say what?" My voice went up to a super high note. "Are you serious? We just took him on a walk two days ago," I countered.

"I know. But his limp. His limp was from a tumor on his hip and they couldn't fix it. And the pain was making him not want to eat. It's so horrible." Tears were streaking down Maia's face now.

My mom put her arm around Maia and gave her a squeeze. "That poor dog. He's probably better off if he was in so much pain, dear."

"I know, that's what Mandi said," Maia mumbled.

"Let me get you a tissue." My mom disappeared into our half bath. I just stood there like a statue. I wasn't sure what to do. I had always made fun of Quince and his big butt, but, now I felt bad. He was a good dog. He was my favorite fat dog.

"What's with all the sad faces?" Sarah said as she bounced down the steps.

"Leave us alone!" I snapped.

"Geez, I was just asking," Sarah growled.

"One of our pets, Quince, died, Sarah," Maia said.

"What happened to him? Was it Paige's fault?"

"NO!" I tried to knock her over with my stare. "He was sick. Now go play with Brian and leave us alone," I said.

Sarah tried to have a stare down with me, but I turned away and ignored her.

"Maia, are you okay?" My mom returned with a tissue.

"Yes. Thank you."

"Come in," my mom said.

"Yea, duh. Come on." I motioned her to follow me. "Let's go up to my room."

Maia slumped down on my bed and wiped her eyes. "I can't believe poor Quince is gone," she sighed.

"I know. He was such a good dog. Except when he refused to walk. Maybe that's why. Maybe his hip has been hurting him for a long time. What if this is our fault? Why didn't we say anything before?" I said.

"We had no idea. Mandi didn't even know he was sick. It just happened so fast she said." Maia blew her nose.

"Should I be crying too?" I said sinking into the bed next to Maia.

"You don't have to. I don't know why I'm so upset," Maia said.

"Yea, why are you so upset?"

Maia shrugged. "Kinda reminds me of when I lost my grandpa. He got sick too."

"He didn't have a bad hip, did he?" The words came out so fast and I couldn't take them back.

"Actually, he did," Maia said.

"Wow. What a coinkydink. Your grandpa wasn't a fat beagle though, was he?" I nudged Maia's shoulder trying to make her laugh.

She shook her head. "No, but still. I miss him. And I'm going to miss walking Quince."

"I know, me too." I put my arm around her and gave her a one-arm hug.

We sat on my bed in silence for a few minutes. I didn't know what else to say. At that moment I was glad I had never lost anyone before. It makes your chest achy. Poor Maia must feel way worse than me.

I jumped to my feet as a grand idea sprang through my mind. "I know what we can do."

Maia looked at me with a wrinkled forehead.

"We should dedicate our float to Quince."

"That's an awesome idea. But how?"

"Well, I don't know. You're the smart one," I said.

"We can write his name on the float real big," Maia said.

"Maybe. Is there a way to do that without ruining it?" I said.

"We can hold a banner up," Maia suggested.

"That won't work. One of us has to pull the float and one of us needs to hold Sandy's leash. Man, now I feel bad I told Quince he couldn't be in the parade because he was too slow." I plopped back onto the bed.

"How about we still make a huge poster with Quince's picture, but we attach it to the float like a flag, so everyone can see it from the top of the doghouse," Maia said.

"Yes, yes. I have poster board we can use. Oh, but where are we going to get a picture of Quince?"

"Everyone takes pictures of their pets. Mandi will have one. We just have to ask for it," Maia said padding her eyes dry.

"Oh, that's kinda weird. You think she'll be freaked out?" I said biting on the tip of my fingernail, already getting nervous about asking her.

"Probably not. Especially since it's like we are honoring him. It'll be a nice thing," Maia said.

"Yea, you're right," I said. "Okay, I'll get the poster started and you ask for the picture."

"You're not going to make me go alone to ask for his picture. No way." Maia shook her head vigorously.

"Okay. We'll go together. It'll be fine. No big deal, right?"

"You girls alright in there?" my mom called through my door.

"Yes, Mom. We'll be out in a minute," I answered.

I took Maia by the arm and eased her up off the bed. "Come on. Let's get this over with."

"I can send her a text first to tell her we are coming," Maia blurted.

"Totally. Great idea. That way it won't be weird when we show up."

"What should I type?" Maia asked, taking out her phone.

"Just type, 'Can we have a picture of Quince so we can dedicate our float to him?' She'll think it's sweet, right?" I said.

"I hope," Maia said as she typed. "Okay. Sent. Now we just wait, I guess."

Mandi finally responded to Maia thirty minutes later. We had our new plan. Our float would officially be dedicated to Quince.

We wanted to go to Mandi's right away and get it over with, but we ended up walking slow like someone was holding onto our shirts trying to keep us from going forward. Approaching Mandi's door knowing Quince wouldn't be there waiting for us was the worst part. My legs felt like rubber bands. It was almost worse than waiting for Max to charge after me with his razor-sharp fangs. Okay, maybe not quite that bad, but pretty close. Maia and I locked arms and knocked together. Mandi was so sweet that I'm not sure why we were nervous. She also paid us for our last few walks. We tried not to take the money, but she insisted.

We decided to use the money to pay to have Quince's picture blown up real big. I wasn't even super bummed that I wouldn't have the extra money to put towards a cell phone.

I did another brave thing. I volunteered to stay home with Sarah and Brownie while my mom went to the store to have the photo enlarged. It wasn't as painful as it sounds. Brownie boy was napping and my dad was in his office. I just had to stir the spaghetti sauce a few times and keep Sarah out of the snacks.

"What are you doing?" I snuck up behind Sarah.

"Nothing."

"Don't lie. You were reaching for the cookies. Mom said no snacks," I said.

"You're not the boss of me," Sarah said.

"Oh yes, I am. I'll tell Mom and you won't get dessert."

"You are so mean. Dad! Paige is being mean!"

"If we bother Dad while he is on a phone call, you'll be the one in trouble, not me, so, ha," I said in her face.

"But I'm hungry," Sarah whined.

"You're just bored."

"Then play with me, Paige. Please!"

I rolled my eyes and let out a huge breath. "Fine. Go pick out a board game," I said.

The torture of playing with Sarah didn't last an eternity. My mom came home after our second game. I was even nice and let Sarah win. Awesome big sister points right here!

"Mom, the picture looks awesome!" I shouted.

"I got an extra in case something happens or if you want a picture on both sides of the poster," my mom said.

"Good idea. I didn't think of that. People will be on both sides of the street." She is always on top of this stuff. MOTHERS!

"How is Maia?" my mom asked.

"She's okay. The poster idea helped cheer her up. I'm going to my room to finish it."

"Can I help?" Sarah bounced up and down.

"Nope." I spun on my heals and darted up the steps.

I just finished gluing down Quince's pictures when my dad popped his head into my room. "Need help attaching that poster to your float?" he asked.

"Yes, please," I said. "It should be dry any minute."

"Okay. There is some extra wood left over. I'm going to go cut some pieces so we can attach the poster, then we can nail it to the top of the roof," my dad said.

"Sure, thanks." I couldn't picture it, but I had to trust he knew what he was doing. "I'll bring it down."

I carried the poster to the garage where my dad was already working his magic. "Hand me the poster. I've got special screws I can use to hold it in place," he said.

If you say so, I thought. Screws in a poster? This didn't sound right. I sat on the little stool that went to my dad's tool bench and just watched. I couldn't wait for Mandi to see the poster. I hope it doesn't make her sad.

"Oh my gosh!" I blurted out.

"What's the matter?" my dad asked.

"Gunther. We totally forgot about Gunther."

"Gunther is..."

"He's the rabbit we are pet sitting. With everything going on today we forgot to feed him."

"Well, go. Before it gets dark. I'll have this done by the time you get back."

"Thanks, Dad."

I stopped at Maia's house to see if she wanted to come with me. "She's out shopping with her grandmother. She thought it would cheer her up," Maia's mom said.

I should have known. Her grandma always takes her shopping. My grandma doesn't cheer me up by buying me things. She just cracks crazy jokes that I totally don't get.

"Um. Can you just let her know my dad is putting the poster on our float and to come see it in the morning?" I said before leaving.

When I went into the house to check on Gunther, I heard a strange scratching sound. For a second, I was scared to move, but when I listened closely, I could tell it was coming from Gunther's cage. Poor guy must be digging his way out.

"Oh, Gunther. I am so sorry we forgot about you," I said. "What are you doing you silly rabbit?"

All his hay was pushed to one end of the cage again. When I bent down to unlock the cage, Gunther looked up at me and twitched his nose.

"I'm here, Gunther. You can go hop around now. And I'll get you some yummy veggies."

I put Gunther in the kitchen and hurried to get his food. Poor bunny was probably starving.

"Go on, hop around while I fill your water," I said. But Gunther just sat there like a big, round hair ball. He was looking extra full and round today. His little pink nose just kept on going. "Or just sit there. It's up to you."

I took care of the nasty part of the job before putting more food in the cage. I folded up the papers with Gunther's little rabbit poop and pee on it. I was going to smooth out the hay again, but then I thought I better not. Apparently, he likes it piled up. And it makes cleaning easier. I scrubbed my hands even though I was sure I didn't touch any of his droppings. That would be ICK!

I filled his water, gave him fresh celery and lettuce, and left the rabbit food that was still in the cage. Then I sat on the floor next to Gunther and pet his head, rubbing his ears. He didn't move. He just sat there. How boring, I thought. No one to talk to him or play with him all day. I was bored just sitting there for two minutes.

After about ten minutes I said, "Alright Gunther, sorry to do this buddy, but you gotta go back in your cage. I have to go home." I was eager to see what my dad had done to the poster.

I locked up Gunther. He looked at me like he was pleading for me not to leave. I stuck my finger into the cage and pet his little nose one last time and said, "I'll be back tomorrow morning."

Sunday, July 4

I woke up to *tap, tap, tap* on the window. I rolled out of bed hoping my suspicions were erroneous. I peeked out the window. GRRR!

"Paige! It's raining outside!" Sarah yelled through my door.

"I know. Go away!"

This could not be happening. I saw nothing but gray clouds and streaks of rain on the glass. What if they cancel the parade? All our hard work would be for nothing.

I ran downstairs. "Is it supposed to rain all day?" I squealed.

My mom said, "No idea. But the parade is rain or shine, as long as it's not thunder and lightning."

"Really? OMG, what if all the paint washes off our float?"

73

"It'll be fine, Paige. Don't worry." My mom's reassurance and sunny disposition was not working on me. She didn't have a year's supply of ice cream at stake.

Maia came to my house to see the float before we walked over to feed Gunther. It looked FANTASTICALLY AWESOME; EAT-OUR-GLITTERY-DUST-ASHLEY AWESOME!

Now, the rain had to stop so it would stay that way.

We popped open our umbrellas and scampered over to see Gunther.

"What did your grandma buy you this time?" I asked as we skipped over puddles.

"Just a cute backpack purse," Maia said.

"Cool. What color?"

"Red. Oh, and a dangly charm to hang off of it. It's a dog charm," Maia added.

"You are so lucky. That sounds so cute," I said, just a little jealous.

We shook out our umbrellas before we went inside and left them on the floor by the door.

"You hear that?" Maia said.

"No, what?"

"Listen. It's a little squeaky sound," Maia said.

"Probably just Gunther. He was scratching at the cage yesterday." I shrugged. "Let's go see."

Holy cow! I thought it before I said it. "Holy cow!"

Maia and I both looked at each other. Our jaws seemed to come unhinged.

"Wha, wha, what in the world?" I said.

"Babies?" Maia said.

"But, he's a boy," I squealed.

"Obviously, the pet store got *that* wrong," Maia said.

"What do we do? What do we do?" I said.

We could barely see the babies. They were in a football-type huddle in the corner of the cage, nestled in the hay and some mulch. The newspaper that was down for Gunther to go to the bathroom on was all shredded and part of the pile the babies were squirming around on.

"EW, they look sort of weird, don't they?" I said.

"I know. Like little bald mice," Maia added.

We stood there just staring at the squirming babies. Every now and then they made a weird squeak. Gunther was at the other end of the cage.

"Why is he, I mean she, ignoring the babies?" I said.

"No idea," Maia said. "Wait, I can look this up on my phone. The internet has everything."

"If I had a phone, I would have thought of that," I groaned.

Maia typed away on her phone as I just watched the babies squish together. Gunther (or maybe we should change his name now that he's a she) was just licking her fur. The whole situation was odd.

"Okay. I think I finally found something," Maia blurted out. "Babies need to be super warm or they will die."

"What? We can't let them die. Why doesn't he, I mean she, sit on them or something with all her fluffy hair?" I was annoyed already.

"Hold on. Still reading."

I leaned over Maia's shoulder so I could read too but she was scrolling too fast. She was like a speed reader. I could be searching for information too...if I had a phone. GRRR!

"It says that we should make a warm basket for them. We need to heat up some towels and put them in it. We don't have a box, but we can use a bowl." Maia was half talking to me and half reading.

"So, we just start going through their house looking for stuff to use?" I griped.

"I don't think we have a choice," Maia said. "I will send them a text message and let them know Gunther is a girl and had babies."

"Will they starve?" I watched the wrinkly, hairless babies wiggle.

"It said that the mother will feed the babies, but only like once or twice a day. We need to keep them alive though," Maia talked as she typed. She was so efficient. She was super pet sitter with her phone that held all the knowledge.

As Maia continued to type I wandered back into the kitchen looking for something to help the situation. How big of a bowl do we need? I had no idea. I peeked inside a few cabinets until I found a stack of plastic bowls.

"How many babies are there?" I hollered to Maia.

I kept my hand on the bowls as I waited for an answer. I assumed she was counting.

"Six," Maia finally shouted back.

I picked the plastic bowl that looked large enough for six pinkish baby bunnies. I moved my fist around the bowl to make sure they could all squeeze in.

"I found a bowl. Now what?" I asked Maia when I returned to the cage.

"Waiting to get a message back from the family. Hoping they have a heating pad. The website says we can use a heating pad wrapped in towels to get them warm."

"Well, we should do something while we wait," I said.

Maia just stared at her phone. I know she was having a rough day yesterday and all, but today is a new day and a new crisis. I needed her. I guess she was doing something by looking up the information, but I felt stupid just standing there holding an empty bowl staring at Maia staring at her phone.

"What if we put some dish towels in the microwave? That will warm them up. Then we can at least get these little guys bundled up for a bit."

"Sure, try that," Maia mumbled.

Okay. I was on it. I found three dish towels and put them in the microwave for three minutes. WOW, they were hot. I quickly put them in the bowl and brought it all back to the cage.

"Okay, I will hold the bowl and you place the babies in it and then I'll cover them with the other towels." Was I the one taking charge?

"What?" Maia looked at me sort of clueless.

"Babies. Pick them up and put them in the bowl," I repeated. I waved a hand in front of Maia's face and snapped my fingers. "Earth to Maia. Babies. Lift from cage before these towels are no longer hot."

"Oh, Yea, sorry. I was just thinking about how these..."

"Think later," I said.

Maia took a deep breath and opened the cage. Gunther didn't budge. I took two towels from the bowl and left one lining the bottom of it. Maia scooped up the babies one at a time and placed them in the bowl. It didn't faze her to pick them up. They didn't even look like bunnies. I hurried up and touched one. It just felt like skin. It squeaked. When the last bunny was in the bowl, I covered them up with the other warm towels.

"What if they can't breathe?" I said.

"I read that they will be fine. Just leave a little gap so air gets in. We need to put the bowl back in the cage so Gunther can eventually feed them," Maia said.

"Guntherette," I said.

"What?"

"It's a little more girly, don't ya think?" I laughed.

"We'll have to come back later to make sure they are okay and still warm," Maia said.

"What about the parade? We can't miss the parade," I said.

"We can't let anyone else die either, Paige. Geez." Maia nearly bit my head off.

"I don't want them to die, either. I was just saying."

"Sorry, I just don't want any more pets dying. That's more important than the parade," Maia sniffled, holding back tears. I could see them forming.

"You're right. We can come back in a little while after the parade is over and then again after the picnic and stuff."

"I may not even go to the parade," Maia said.

"Say what, now?" I was shocked.

"I'm not in the mood."

"Maia, we worked so hard on our float. Plus, we have it dedicated to Quince. You can't just ignore that. He was an awesomely fat dog who deserves to be remembered," I said. "And, I can't walk Sandy and pull a float alone."

"I know, but so much is going on now and it might still be raining when the parade starts. It's like a sign that we shouldn't be going to the parade."

"The rain sucks, but the parade is rain or shine. If you don't do this for Quince, then at least do this so I can rub it in know-it-all Ashley's face because we are so gonna win," I pleaded.

"You are crazy, you know that?" Maia cracked a tiny smile.

"I will do it for Quince. That's it. Then I will go home after the parade."

"What? You can't. What about the movie in the park? You're ruining the Fourth of July for me."

"And you're being selfish, Paige."

"You are too, you know. But, go ahead. Go home and sulk if that makes you feel better, even though it won't bring Quince back or help keep these bunnies alive, but go ahead. I'll watch the movie all alone and eat all the candy myself." I wasn't sure if I was trying to make her feel guilty or like she was going to miss out on all the fun. Either way, it wasn't working.

"What if I promise we'll come back to check on the bunnies one more time before the movie starts? Then will you come? Pleeeeease," I said curling my fingers together in her face as I begged.

"We have to check on them after the fireworks too," Maia said.

"Fine, but only if someone comes with us. It'll be late."

"You are such a chicken," Maia teased.

"I don't deny it. Now, will you please say you won't abandon me today?"

"I won't abandon you today," Maia said.

"YAY! Now, let's get moving. Guntherette, we'll be back to check on you later. Now feed those babies," I said.

"Let me just peek in on them before we go," Maia said.

She unlatched the cage. Guntherette didn't bother to try and escape. She lifted the towel and I peeked over the top of the cage.

"They aren't moving around anymore. Are they, you know, dead?" I whispered.

Maia touched one of them with her finger. "Still warm. The website said that they move around a lot and squirm together when they are too cold, so they must be warming up if they are calm."

"Phew. Cover them back up so they don't get chilled," I said.

"Look!" I shouted when we got outside. "The sun is coming out. Oh, please let the sun stay out."

"You are losing it," Maia laughed.

"I just can't wait to win a year of free ice cream. It'll be so awesome," I said closing my umbrella.

Maia finally smiled a real smile. A big, mouth-full-of-braces-covered-teeth smile. "We can try all their flavors, a different one every day," she said.

"OMG! I can't wait. What time should we pick up Sandy?" I said.

"The Youngs sent me a message saying they are going to the parade, so they will bring Sandy with them and come find us."

Of course, Maia got a message and I didn't. Soon, hopefully, I'll have my own message machine; a.k.a. a cell phone.

"Well, that's easy," I said. "Now we just worry about getting our float there."

It wasn't easy avoiding Sarah once I got home. She was on my heels as soon as I walked in the door.

"Paige, Paige," Sarah barked in my ear. I tried to ignore her, but she just wouldn't stop. "Paige, Paige, Paige."

"WHAT!" I shouted.

"Hey, your brother is sleeping, keep it down. I don't want him crabby for the parade," my mom scolded.

I scrunched my face together and stared at Sarah. It felt like lasers were coming out of my eyes. Now, that would be a great power to have. I could zap whatever I wanted. Okay, I didn't want to zap Sarah, but it would be cool. I just wanted her to leave me alone.

"Go away!" I mouthed.

Apparently, Sarah can't read lips. She followed me to the bathroom.

"Privacy, please." I shut the door in her face.

"Can I please walk in the parade with you? Please," she begged from the other side of the door.

"No way," I said.

"You are so mean." I heard her foot stomp on the floor.

"If you leave me alone, I'll take you to see the new bunnies," I grumbled.

"Really? What new bunnies?" Sarah shrieked.

"Gunther is really a girl and had babies. Now go away."

"Cool," Sarah said. Then I heard her walk away. That should keep her off my back for a while. I paced in the garage as I waited for Maia to show up. What was taking her so long?

It was like a half mile to the parade. And we only had an hour before it started. I looked over the float. It looked great. No one would miss the poster of Quince. I had a bucket filled with candy to toss to the crowd and was wearing my new Critter Sitter shirt. I was ready to go! Except, Maia was a no-show!

We had gone to check on the bunnies like I promised. They were fine, Maia seemed fine too. So, I started to get agitated when I looked at my watch.

My mom peeked her head out the door and asked, "You're still here?"

"Yep. Not sure what is taking Maia so long," I sighed.

"Why don't you just run down to her house and get her?" my mom said.

"I'm keeping an eye on the float. I don't want Sarah touching it."

"I'll make sure she doesn't," my mom said.

I hesitated. I walked around the float a few times to make sure nothing was wrong with it and then looked at my watch again. Then I started down the driveway. I looked back over my shoulder to make sure my mom was on the job. She was still standing at the door. She better not move.

Just as I started towards Maia's I saw her curls waving as she sprinted towards me. Her Critter Sitter shirt was tied in a knot just like mine. BFFs do think alike.

"What in the world took so long?" I said when she reached me.

"One of my sandals broke, can you believe it? My grandma just bought them for me. And then I couldn't find one of my tennis shoes and then my mom made me eat a sandwich and then I got a call about Gunther and..."

"Guntherette," I corrected her.

"Whatever, that's too hard to remember," Maia said.

"I know, it sounds weird, but what did they say? Talk as we walk, we gotta get going."

When we got back into the garage it took a second for me to realize my mom was no longer keeping a protective watch over our float. GRRR!

"You guide the back while I pull it forward until we get it straight on the sidewalk," I said to Maia.

It seemed positively sturdy, but we were very cautious as we rolled it down to the sidewalk.

"So, what happened with the bunny call?" I finally remembered Maia hadn't finished telling me.

"Oh, right! There are cousins that live forty-minutes from here. They've got like a mini farm going on at their house so they're coming to pick up the babies. We don't have to worry about them," Maia explained.

"What about Gunther...ette?"

"He's...she's going too. For a while, I guess, because she has to feed the babies. Then they'll get her back at some point."

"Interesting. I don't know anyone with a farm."

"Me either," Maia said.

"Kind of stinks though. That means no more pet sitting money for us. Actually, that's two less jobs, now." I huffed like a disgruntled employee. But then my voice saddened. "I mean, I guess we'll have to find some new pets. But, not to replace you, Quince," I said looking at his poster.

"Someone else will need us," Maia said. "Until we get another call, we'll just get done sooner and can have more free time." Brightside Maia was back. "I'm just glad the bunnies will be okay."

"Me too," I said.

"AHH!" we both shouted as the wagon rattled over a large broken piece of concrete. We let out huge sighs of relief when the doghouse didn't fall off the wagon.

"My dad put this thing on good. We have nothing to worry about," I declared.

"Totally," Maia said.

When we arrived at the starting point of the parade there was a swarm of people and floats galore!

"WOW! Look at all these floats. Some are really, really good. OMG, look at that pirate ship one." It was overwhelming.

"It's good, but what does a pirate ship have to do with July Fourth, anyway?" Maia said.

"True. But, it's still cool."

"Over there." Maia pointed. "We need to go to that table to check in."

I followed Maia and pulled the wagon behind me trying to weave carefully around people. Precious cargo coming through, people, watch out!

The lady welcoming float contestants gave us a sticker with the number thirty-two on it. "Place this on your float so it can be judged accurately," she told us. Then she put little checkmarks next to our names on a list she had attached to a clipboard. This was official stuff.

"How many floats are there?" I asked the lady.

"We limited it to fifty, but only forty signed up," she said.

"Oh, wow, we are close to the end of the parade, Maia," I said. "Is that good or bad?"

"It doesn't matter, everyone always watches the entire parade," the lady answered for Maia.

Maia took the sticker and said, "Thank you."

"That sticker is going to make our float look weird," I griped.

"Everyone has to do it. We'll put it over the little dog door, so it looks like the doghouse address," Maia said. Brilliant. As always!

After we put the sticker on the doghouse I realized I had forgotten to put the stuffed dog inside the float door. I shook it off trying to remain positive. With Sandy and the poster of Quince, maybe no one would notice the doghouse was empty.

Maia asked another parade walker who had five pounds of beads around her neck to take our picture with the float. One more reason I need a phone; instant pictures at my fingertips. The lady took two pictures.

"Super cute," she said as she handed Maia her phone back.

Maia spotted the Youngs in the crowd and waved them over. They handed us Sandy's leash and wished us luck. We tied a patriotic Fourth of July bandana around her neck and she licked my hand. Her licks were much more tolerable than monster Max's. This was a good decision to walk with Sandy.

Maia gave Sandy a treat then turned on her dog whisperer voice and said, "You can have another one after our walk, okay? Good girl."

I don't know how she does it. I would sound so foolish.

A couple people told us they liked our float. That pumped us up. A high-five was in order.

"Don't look now."

Maia scanned the crowd. "Don't look where? At who?" she whispered.

"Don't look, I said. You look like you're looking for someone. Stop it," I said out of the corner of my mouth.

"Who am I not supposed to look for?" Maia's eyes bulged at me.

"Ashley. She's right over... Oh, hey Ashely," I said as she appeared right in front of us. My lips were squeezed closed so I wouldn't burst into laughter. Her outfit was...unexpected. No, something this extravagant was expected from Ashley. It was horrific.

Ashley was dressed like the Statue of Liberty. She was all wrapped up in a green sheet and her face was painted. Not very smoothly either. She was carrying a torch made from a flashlight and construction paper. It flickered like a green glowing flame. GRRR! It was over the top. Way too much. I kind of felt bad for her. The sun had finally come out and it was getting warm. She might pass out wrapped up the way she was, and that makeup was bound to melt right off her face. I was not feeling sorry for her. She looked good...for now. But all I thought was, it's a good thing she's already green because she'll be green with envy once we win.

"So, this is your float?" Ashley said.

"It looks that way doesn't it?" I replied.

"Where is yours, Ashley?" Maia asked politely.

"Oh, mine is that big one over there with the star made out of balloons and the flag made from carnations."

Carnations? Really? How many flowers would die for her float?

"Cute shirts, but they aren't very patriotic," Ashely said.

"They're part of our business plan. It's called advertisement," I said.

"Okay, well good luck then. You're gonna need it," Ashley said and tossed her straight Statue of Liberty hair over her shoulder.

"We're just here to have fun, Ashley," Maia said.

My head whipped in Maia's direction and I glared hard. We were not here just for fun. This was a competition.

"Okay. Well, see ya after the parade," Ashley said and spun around in her green shoes. She was even wearing green shoes.

"Why did you say that?" I sputtered when Ashley and her green ears were far enough away. "We came to win."

"But look at all these floats, Paige. We better just have fun because we might not win." Maia crushed my spirit.

"Fine, if you wanna be that way. I think our float is awesome though."

"It is, but we shouldn't get our hopes up is all I'm saying," Maia shrugged.

"We have to win, for Quince," I said.

Maia looked up at Quince's photo on top of our float. "You're right. He would have loved a year's supply of ice cream," Maia said with a smile.

Someone with a clipboard and a megaphone made an announcement to all parade walkers to leave space between the floats. Don't walk too fast and don't walk too slow. If we have anything for the crowd it needs to be gently tossed or handed out. No sharp objects, no flammable objects, no exiting the parade line through the crowd with your float. We must take it all the way to the end. Wow, these were a lot of rules. I never knew so much went into putting on a good town parade. I was startled by the sound of drums. It sounded like a marching band was leading the way. I didn't see any of that when we arrived. We were really towards the end of the procession.

When it was our turn to start walking, I pulled the float and Maia held Sandy's leash. Sandy was a model citizen. She walked so nicely next to us. Whenever we saw someone in the crowd with a pet, we tossed them a treat from our bucket and

Maia tossed candy to little kids. It felt weird parading down the street. People were waving at us like we're famous. We waved back even though we didn't know most of them.

"Hey Paige! Maia! Over here! Throw me some candy!" Sarah's voice screeched from the rows of people. I spotted my dad with Brownie on his shoulders. I waved to them and threw Sarah one piece of candy. I knew she would be annoyed I only gave her one piece, but we still had a long way to go and lots of votes to win.

We made a turn down Market Street. I quickly dropped my hand to my side and tried hard to look straight ahead. I was overcome with stage fright. I know I wasn't on a stage, but it felt like I was. Eyes looking right at me, his particularly. Judging my every move as I waved like a silly person. My eyes focused on the float in front of us. Nevertheless, I could still see him standing in the sea of people on the left side of the street sweeping his hair out of his eye. YIKES! This is what I wanted, right? For Ryan to come back from his boat house. I wasn't so sure anymore.

If he was in the crowd, he wasn't in the parade with Ashley. Maia was right. She had lied.

Maia looked at me and said, "You need to toss out some more candy, Paige."

"Oh yea. Okay. Okay."

I took a handful of candy from the other bucket and tossed it at the crowd quickly. Some of it went right towards Ryan but I didn't make eye contact. I couldn't. This was so embarrassing.

"Not so hard," Maia scolded under her breath.

A few more feet and he wouldn't see us anymore, I told myself. I tossed a few more pieces, more gently, then asked Maia if she wanted to switch.

"Oh, hey look, there's Mandi," Maia said. We waved to her and she blew us a kiss then wiped her eyes. It must have been sad to see big ol' Quince up on display. Then we saw Buster's family. Buster's tail was going a mile a minute. Just a few feet away was Mrs. Henderson. She was sitting in a canvas fold-out chair right up front. Sitting like a gentleman right next to her was Max. His tongue was flapping to the side of his jaw. From the street I could see the pointed ends of his ferocious man-eating teeth.

"Hi girls," Mrs. Henderson said as we came closer to her. Max jumped to his three feet when he spotted us. I could see Mrs. Henderson had a leash on him, but when I looked down it wasn't hooked to the chair. Mrs. Henderson must have dropped it when she raised her arm and waved. I could see the hunger in Max's eyes as he sprang into action.

Mrs. Henderson stood but her legs were not fast enough for Max. I was sort of relieved when Max went to Maia. He sniffed her frantically.

"He wants a you-know-what," I said. "Give me Sandy and just give him one so he leaves us alone."

Sandy's leash quickly swapped hands, leaving me with a leash in one hand and the handle to the float in the other. We were still walking at a snail pace trying to appease Max and keep up with the crowd. Maia dug a treat out of the treat bucket so Max would eat it and leave. He chewed the treat for less than a second then sniffed Sandy who was easily excited.

Her tail was wagging like a signal that said, "Here I am, come play with me, Max." The two dogs hadn't seen each other since my not-so-brilliant idea to take all the dogs on a walk together, but apparently, they recognized each other, and are not familiar with phrases like, this is not the time to become reacquainted. What I really was thinking was, why hasn't anyone come to retrieve Max and get him out of the way?

Max was about to weave under Sandy's leash and become tangled. That's why I shouted, "No, Max, no!"

His head snapped quickly my way as if he just noticed I was there. No, no, no! I screamed in my head. My voice extinguished his interest in Sandy. His two front paws sprung into the air. As always, they landed right on my chest. He barked loudly and his nasty dog spit sprayed across my face. He was just getting me seasoned for a tasty bite.

The parade float walkers that were in front of us had continued on. So now we were just standing in the street with all eyes on us. I'm sure everyone could see the fear on my face and think I wasn't capable of getting dogs under control. But I was defenseless with my hands full. I could feel Max's razor-sharp teeth getting closer.

I dropped Sandy's leash so I could guard my face and shove Max away. Sandy quickly circled around the float and yelped with excitement. Max pushed off me, eager to join Sandy. I lost my balance and stumbled backwards. I could see Maia out of the corner of my eye chasing Sandy. Max started chasing both of them. That left no one to catch me. Before tumbling onto my back in the middle of the street, I crashed into the doghouse. It toppled over just missing Maia's foot.

At that moment time froze. Nobody moved. Nobody said a word. The crowd's cheers and claps came to an immediate stop. All eyes were on us. Then suddenly, the Youngs showed up in the middle of the street and were able to get Sandy under control. They walked her off to the side of the street. Maia spoke to Max in her dog-whisperer voice and it only took a moment, AND a treat, for him to sit. Maia grabbed him by the collar and led him back to Mrs. Henderson. The rest of the parade walkers and floats started going around us.

Another embarrassing moment, all thanks to Max. GRRR! I didn't even want to get up and keep going. I wanted to just crawl behind a tree and hide. I sat up and with my elbows resting on my bent knees, I hid my face. I needed a moment to catch my composure. Some people asked if I wanted help and said they felt awful for us. I just waved them on without looking up. I was better off just sitting there in self-pity. Then a hand stretched out in front of me. It was attached to someone wearing sporty slide-on sandals. Go away, I thought.

"Hey, you okay? I can help you guys get the float back on the wagon."

Oh no! Don't let it be. Please! I didn't want to look up, but I had to. I quickly used the pads of my hands to wipe my cheeks dry. I couldn't let anyone, especially Ryan, see me cry. I took a deep breath and lifted my head.

"Hey. Can you believe this?" I tried to laugh as I reached for Ryan's hand and used his grip to stand up.

"Why in the world would that lady let her dog loose during the parade?" Ryan said in a tone that totally expressed my frustration.

"Mrs. Henderson didn't mean it. It's hard to control Max. He does whatever he wants," I said dusting off my shorts.

"Are you hurt? I mean, you look okay, but?" Ryan asked.

"I think I'm fine. I'm sure everyone had a good laugh though," I said.

"It was funny, but only for like a second," Ryan said as he bent over to help me tilt the float upright again.

"I just can't believe the entire parade went on without us. I'm sure the float is ruined now anyway," I said.

"Hey, let me help," Maia said jogging toward us. She held onto the wagon as Ryan and I straightened out the doghouse. Poor Quince's poster was bent, but it still looked alright.

"Mrs. Henderson feels awful. Are you okay?" Maia said.

"I guess. Thanks to Ryan," I shyly said.

"You're just an everyday hero, aren't you?" Maia said in a snarky tone. What was her deal? I was the one thrown to the ground in front of a hundred people.

Ryan simply brushed the hair out of his eyes with his hand.

"Are you going to try and catch up to the rest of the parade?" Ryan asked.

Maia and I looked at each other. "Should we?" she asked.

"As long as Max is far out of sight," I said. I looked down at my hands. My palms were red and scraped. "Hopefully I can pull the wagon, though." I held up my hands showing them my battle wounds. Apparently, I was still at war with Max.

"I'll help. I mean, if you want," Ryan said.

"Sure. I'll just toss the candy out if there is anyone still left on the street," I said with a smile.

"Okay, come on. We aren't too far behind," Maia said interrupting my eye contact with Ryan. She took Sandy's leash back from Mr. Young and we continued on.

Most of the crowd had started gathering their chairs and blankets and were walking towards the park. A few started clapping as we began walking again. Not sure if that is cool or pathetic.

"So, um. Ashely told me you were helping her with her float. Why aren't you walking in the parade with her?" I asked Ryan. I couldn't help it. I had to know.

"She said what? Why would I be helping Ashley?" Ryan said.

"I told you she made it all up," Maia said.

"She is ruthless. She just hates me is all. She is always trying to get me mad," I griped.

"So, you'd be mad if I was in the parade with Ashley?" Ryan asked in a teasing way.

"Not mad, really. Just like, whatever. She makes it sound like you guys are like, whatever..." I couldn't get the right words out. "...she is always..."

"She tries to make Paige jealous because she knows Paige likes you," Maia blurted out.

OMG! I wanted to crawl inside the doghouse and hide. Why would Maia say that? My face was hotter than a firecracker.

I said, *Maia, how dare you*, with my eyes as I glared at her over my shoulder.

"Um. What I meant is that she is always lying to us about something," I quickly said.

"Well, I've never talked to her, outside of school, I mean. So, don't worry," Ryan said.

"No one is worried," I said. Not anymore, I thought. I was totally smiling. But they couldn't see it because I was leading our new trio and had my back to them.

We marched down the street quickly trying to catch up with the float in front of us. By the time we did, we were at the park's entrance and the parade was coming to an end. Thankfully, enough people saw our float and would be able to vote on it. I still had hope. My candy bucket was just about empty. Only three pieces remained. I handed both Maia and Ryan a piece and unwrapped the last one for myself.

"I better go find my parents and let them know I'm hanging with you guys," Ryan said as he popped the candy in his mouth.

He's hanging with us? YIKES! I mean that in the best possible way.

"We'll be around. So, if we see you, we see you," Maia said.

I tried to blink away the confusion and the distorted look on my face. What in the world was she saying? I ignored her comment for now and turned to Ryan.

"Thank you for helping us. We'll be here until fireworks start so..."

"Okay, cool." Ryan swept his hair back and walked away.

"What was that about?" I snapped at Maia.

"What are you talking about?"

"You like basically told him we wouldn't hang out with him."

"Why should we?"

"Because he was being nice." As if she didn't know why else.

"This is our day, though. Parade, movie, fireworks, remember?" Maia sounded sad. I know she was still really sad about Quince, so I tried to be sensitive.

"It is. I swear. We have all day to hang together. But he can hang out with us for a little while, can't he? It's not like we are going to just leave you. OMG. I don't want to be alone with him," I said, whispering that last part.

Maia laughed. "So, I'm your buffer?"

"No, yes. Come on. You are my best friend. I need you," I begged.

"Okay, he can hang. Later though. I don't want to be with him all night," Maia said.

"No, totally," I tried to agree, but I was already scanning the park to see where he had disappeared to.

I stood in line with my parents, Sarah, and Brian to buy hamburgers and chips. Maia was already sitting at a table with her mom and dad. It had been an hour since I last saw Ryan. It was like he just vanished.

My mom made me sit with the family to eat. I tried to mouth it to Maia, but I don't think she knew what I was saying.

Suddenly, a voice bellowed through the air. I hadn't even noticed the speaker stands until then. We were told that the movie would start in an hour so it would be over in time for the fireworks show and that they would announce the float winners shortly. That got me all excited.

"Can I please go be with Maia while they announce the winners?" I pleaded with my mom.

"Yes. Brian doesn't like the fireworks, so I am going to take him home right after the movie. Dad will stay with Sarah, so look for him to walk you home."

"I'm not a baby," I said.

"Do you want to keep an eye on Sarah so I can go home early too then," my dad chimed in.

"No way! Where should I meet you?" I sighed like a deflating balloon.

After getting final instructions, I got up to dispose of my trash so I could sit with Maia.

"Hey."

I dropped my paper plate and napkin in the garbage bin and spun. Ryan was at arm's reach.

"Oh hey. Haven't seen you in a while. Maia didn't scare you off, did she?"

"No, I went home and came back. Wanted to pack up a few things before we go back to the boat."

"You're leaving already to go back? Didn't you just get here?" I'm sure I sounded desperate and clingy.

"My dad insists we be there or there is no sense in having it. I totally get it," Ryan said swooshing his hair back.

"How are the fish?" I said.

Ryan stared at me with his eyebrows wrinkled close together. "How'd you know I have fish?"

OOPS! How was I going to get out of this one?

"Well..." I started.

"We're going to announce the winners of the float contest," a voice roared through the speakers.

Phew. Saved by the announcer lady. "OMG! I gotta hear this. Doubt we have a chance. Oh, there's Maia," I said. I saw Maia over Ryan's shoulder. "Come on, we gotta go be with Maia," I said and grabbed Ryan's hand. I hadn't realized I did that until we were done weaving through picnic tables as I pulled him behind me.

"Hey, *you* two," Maia said glancing down at our hands.

OMG! I dropped Ryan's hand quickly and brushed off my embarrassment by clapping really quickly like a giddy child. "Do you think we have a chance? Come on, let's get closer."

"You want me to wait here?" Ryan asked.

"No. No. Come on!" I said, scooping the air between us so he'd follow.

Maia and I found a spot under a tree near the lady making the announcements. We sat down next to each other. We were shoulder to shoulder bracing ourselves for whatever may happen. Ryan sank down and sat on the other side of me.

"I hope you win," Ryan said. "That would be wicked cool. Who's that dog you had on the poster, anyway?"

I leaned over to Ryan and told him about Quince. I didn't want to upset Maia again, so I whispered. "He was a cool fat dog. We're gonna miss him."

"Oh, I remember him. He was pretty fat," Ryan laughed.

"I know, right. So, we dedicated our float to him," I said.

Maia was unusually quiet. I nudged her shoulder and made a *what's up* face. She never responded because the lady in the red shirt said, "Our third-place winner will receive a snow cone machine with a basket of flavoring."

"Oh WOW! That's not a bad gift," I said to Maia.

"It's not, but you already have one," Maia reminded me.

"Oh yea, that would stink. But you'd be able to keep it," I said.

"Team Independence with the hot air balloon float," The lady said with her voice filled with excitement.

That float was pretty cool, but it wasn't as cool as ours, I thought.

"Maybe you'll get second place," Ryan said, nudging my knee with his. I swallowed hard, but pretended it was no big deal.

"I hope we get something." I made a fake nervous smile.

"Second place will get four tickets to Uptown Movie Theatre and a coupon for the concession stand," the lady said. "Second place goes to..."

A dog started barking right next to us. Come on, not now. This is important stuff. I wanna hear!

"Hey, that's your pet from the parade," Ryan said.

I looked over and Sandy was barking at a squirrel up in the tree. Not now, Sandy. I motioned her over so I could pet her and hopefully calm her down.

"She. That's Sandy. She's a she," I said.

Sandy came over to Maia and me and immediately started licking. "Not now girl. Shhh," Maia said. I was too busy focusing on Sandy that I wasn't sure if I heard the second-place winner correctly.

"Did...did she just say Ashley's name?" I asked, looking at Ryan. He nodded his head. I snapped back to Maia. "Are you kidding? Ashley won something? We will never hear the end of this. She will rub it in our faces for eternity," I groaned.

Her float was good. I guess I couldn't knock her design even if it was a bit over the top. Ashley went up to get her prize and waved a little *HA-HA, look at me* wave flashing a green smile that said, *I told you so.* GRRR! When her eyes glanced over and saw Ryan it was obvious she knew she had been outed. All the comments about her friendship with Ryan and being parade partners with him was a big fat lie and she knew I knew.

Ashley tried to rush back to her spot but had to pass by us. She didn't look our way until Maia said, "Congratulations Ashley."

Maia has always had more tolerance for others than me, especially know-it-all Ashley, but I decided to follow Maia's lead. "Yea, Ashley. Congratulations. Hopefully all those flowers don't die right away." Okay. That last part just slipped out. Ashley just swooshed by in her green sheet and didn't say anything back to us. I was shocked.

"Now, for first place. The winner will get free ice cream for a year at Moo Moo's Creamery." The lady with the microphone looked down at her paper and then back at the crowd. Can't she read? Just say it already. "Well, it turns out..."

SAY THE NAMES! I was freaking out inside. Maia and I squeezed each other's hand. I thought it might turn blue we were gripping so tightly.

"We have a tie. Let me just get confirmation..." The lady put her hand over the mic and spoke with a man holding a clipboard. They were bobbing their heads and whispering. It was torture.

"Where do you keep a year's supply of ice cream?" Ryan asked. I wasn't sure if he was joking. I didn't even want to acknowledge his question as I was too focused on this lady with all the power. So, without looking away from the makeshift stage, which was just a picnic table, I quickly said, "You don't keep it. You go to Moo Moo's for a year, every day if you want, and get free ice cream."

"Cool."

Yes. It is very cool, I thought. TELL US ALREADY!

The lady turned her attention back to everyone staring at her and said, "Moo Moo's is a town favorite and loves its customers. It has agreed that they would acknowledge two winning teams. I just wanted to clarify that before announcing any winners."

GRRR! I was going to explode. The lady holding the microphone looked back at her piece of paper and called, "Freedom Fliers."

They were two floats in front of us...before the collision with Max. They were throwing paper airplanes into the audience that were really coupons to a hair salon. This was it. One more name and it was all over. I had honest to goodness butterflies in my stomach. Maia seemed so patient and calm, UNTIL she jumped to her feet nearly tearing my arm out of the socket. "Paige, we won!" Maia shouted.

"Did she really just say, Critter Sitters?" I exclaimed.

"Yes!"

Maia and I hugged while jumping around. That riled up Sandy and she started jumping too. At that point I didn't care. She could jump all she wanted.

We were so stunned that the lady announcing the winners had to say, "Come on up here girls. We know you had a little incident during the parade, but the crowd loved your design and proud dedication to Quince."

Maia and I went up to the fake stage in front of everyone. It was sort of embarrassing. The lady handed us a laminated card on a lanyard. It said: CONGRATULATIONS FICW. Underneath in small print were the words FREE ICE CREAM WINNER. I never would have figured that out. Maia and I high-fived. My cheeks were beginning to hurt from all the smiling. Even Ryan was smiling. I felt as though we were pity winners because our float was not as cool as the Freedom Fliers, but I was too happy to care.

"That's so cool. Congratulations you guys," Ryan said when we went back to our spot under the tree.

"We so have to celebrate with ice cream tomorrow. You in?" I said pointing to Ryan.

"Umm…"

"Maia, this is so awesome. We have to have one cone in honor of Quince," I said not letting Ryan answer.

"Totally. Quince is the reason our float won anyway," Maia said.

The crowd of people started moving all around, throwing away garbage and spreading out blankets for the movie. I almost lost track of what was happening.

"Hey, you guys, since I put the glitter on the float, do I get to share the ice cream too?" I heard Sarah say squeezing through a group of people.

When she was staring up at me, I said, "Maybe I'll treat you to a scoop or two." I'm sure I'll regret those words later because she will ask me first thing in the morning, every morning, for an entire year until I do. But I was too psyched to say no.

As we were finding our place in the grass for the movie, Maia whispered, "Don't you think we should celebrate *our* win tomorrow," pointing a finger back and forth between her and I.

"Of course. I won't bring Sarah. Her nagging may kill me, which would mean more ice cream for you," I joked.

"Okay. So, no Ryan then either," Maia said quickly.

OH! My eyes shot open real wide. I didn't realize she was so, so…I didn't have the right word for it. Was she mad at me for inviting him? Was she jealous? Did she hate him? A fraction of me was crushed. Like my BFF had just dumped our float right on my chest. I thought we had settled all this at the amusement park. I wasn't sure when I'd see him again this summer and she was ruining my last chance.

"Well, I was going to tell him to bring Corey. But, if you think it should be just us, then I guess it's fine."

"Corey is nice and all, but..."

"But what?" I nudged her.

"I don't really like him, like him," Maia said scrunching her face.

"Oh, you are gonna break his poor silent heart," I laughed.

"Don't make me sound so mean," Maia said.

"I'm not."

Suddenly, the nearby streetlights went dark and everyone hushed. Darkness was settling in. Maia quickly tossed her blanket on the ground and we sat down before the people behind us started to get annoyed. I saw Sarah in the distance talking to my dad and pointing towards me. I knew she was asking if she could come sit with us, but I saw my dad shake his head. Sarah crossed her arms and pouted. That just confirmed it.

Critter Sitter Chronicles 2: 4th of July Parade

The crowd of people got quiet as the movie started. The sun was down, but it was still warm outside, like most July nights. The clouds made the sky seem darker, which made it seem later than it really was. I hoped it wouldn't rain and ruin the fireworks.

Maia and I sat staring at the large movie screen. My mind kept wandering off. Victory felt so good. I hadn't seen Ashley to rub it in her face. I decided to follow in Maia's footsteps and be nice to her about it anyway. It was going to be hard, but I was going to try.

I couldn't decide which flavor I would eat first. Would I try a different one each day? Decisions, decisions. I couldn't imagine eating ice cream for free for an entire year. I wondered if I would get sick of it. No way!

I felt a breeze across my arm as someone sat next to me. I looked over and tried not to let my excitement show.

"Hi," I whispered to Ryan. "I thought you left."

"No. I wanted to see the movie," he said.

Maia seemed to be so focused on the movie she didn't notice Ryan sitting there.

"Hey," Ryan leaned over and whispered in my ear. It gave me goosebumps! "Why'd you ask me about my fish earlier? How'd you know, that like I have fish?"

BUSTED! Okay, this was not the time or the place to tell him, but I couldn't lie to him. He has been so sweet. I took a deep breath before leaning his way.

"I am, we are, um, sorta your pet sitters. Your mom hired us before you left for your lake house, or boat house, or whatever it is. I wasn't sure if you knew or not."

Okay, that part was a lie. Of course, he didn't know. Why else would he be asking?

"So, you like come to our house every day? Why didn't you tell me?"

"I don't know. Maia goes most days, but I do come sometimes to feed them," I said between my teeth.

"Did something happen to them? Their tank was a little dirty when we got back," Ryan said.

"No, um, the fish were fine, but...the—"

"SHHH!" Someone sitting behind us shushed us. I was saved from going into detail about the filter. Or staring at his picture. Or the time I dropped the key in the tank. I quickly leaned over and said, "Sorry I didn't tell you. I thought it might be weird."

Maia shot us a glare that said, *Zip It!* Wow! Okay, I was going to be quiet.

I made an *OOPS* face at Ryan and mouthed the word sorry. I faced the movie, but I didn't hear a word the actors were saying. All I kept wondering was if Ryan was mad and what if he didn't like me anymore.

Great, was that a raindrop I felt on my forehead? I looked up out of instinct and got another drop of rain right in the eye. This day was going from awesome to mood-killer really quick. I wiped my face and said, "Oh this is great," not realizing I said it aloud.

"It's just water," Ryan said and crept his hand across the ground and weaved his fingers between mine. His hand was super warm. Mine must have felt like a sweaty armpit, but I didn't let go. At that point, I lost all interest in the movie.

"You want to leave?" Maia whispered.

"Not yet. It might just drizzle. Let's see what happens," I whispered back and pretended to watch the movie. And what happened was, the rain passed and Ryan held my hand until the fireworks show was over. I couldn't tell if the pounding in my chest was from the exploding firework booms or my heart.

Monday, July 5: The day after victory!

Ryan was off to his boat house again and Maia and I were back to work. We walked the dogs extra fast so we could get to Moo Moo's Creamery and enjoy our sweet victory for the first time. We were down two jobs; the Shootie's fed their fish before they left again for the lake (which means Maia got her way and Ryan wouldn't be joining us for ice cream), and Quince was eternally resting peacefully. Maia was on Max duty today. I was not letting his wet, stinky tongue anywhere near my Ryan-hand-holding hand again! Not like the time after Adventure Park.

When we got to Moo Moo's Creamery, we both celebrated with a double scoop (Cookie Crunch for me and Gooey Peanut Butter for Maia), hot fudge, whipped cream, and sprinkles. Maia took a selfie of us on her phone. It was priceless. Maybe before the summer is over, I'll finally have my own phone and *I'll* be able to take the pictures…I hope!

Valerie is the author of **Returning Santa's Boot, Lila Lies and Critter Sitter Chronicles.** She resides with her family in Nebraska and has always had a passion for writing. She gets most of her children and middle grade story inspiration from her daughters. Find out what's coming next at www.norellapress.com.

www.ingramcontent.com/pod-product-compliance
Lightning Source LLC
Chambersburg PA
CBHW030544130626
46552CB00006B/2411